MW00331345

Bloody Commas 2

T.J. Edwards

Lock Down Publications and Ca$h
Presents
Bloody Commas 2
A Novel by *T.J. Edwards*

Bloody Commas 2

Lock Down Publications
Po Box 870494
Mesquite, Tx 75187

Copyright 2017 by Bloody Commas 2 T.J. Edwards

All rights reserved. No part of this book may be reproduced in any form or by electronic or mechanical means, including information storage and retrieval systems without permission in writing from the publisher, except by a reviewer who may quote brief passages in review.
First Edition December 2017
Printed in the United States of America

This is a work of fiction. Names, characters, places, and incidents either are products of the author's imagination or are used fictitiously. Any similarity to actual events or locales or persons, living or dead, is entirely coincidental.

Lock Down Publications
**Like our page on Facebook: Lock Down Publications
@**
www.facebook.com/lockdownpublications.ldp
Cover design and layout by: **Dynasty Cover Me**
Book interior design by: **Shawn Walker**
Edited by: **Shawn Walker**

Stay Connected with Us!

Text **LOCKDOWN** to 22828 to stay up-to-date with new releases, sneak peaks, contests and more...
Or CLICK HERE to sign up.

Thank you!

Like our page on Facebook:

Lock Down Publications: Facebook

Join Lock Down Publications/The New Era Reading Group

Follow us on Instagram:

Lock Down Publications: Instagram

Email Us: We want to hear from you!

Submission Guideline.

Submit the first three chapters of your completed manuscript to ldpsubmissions@gmail.com, subject line: Your book's title. The manuscript must be in a .doc file and sent as an attachment. Document should be in Times New Roman, double spaced and in size 12 font. Also, provide your synopsis and full contact information. If sending multiple submissions, they must each be in a separate email.

Have a story but no way to send it electronically? You can still submit to LDP/Ca$h Presents. Send in the first three chapters, written or typed, of your completed manuscript to:

LDP: Submissions Dept
Po Box 870494
Mesquite, Tx 75187

DO NOT send original manuscript. Must be a duplicate.

Provide your synopsis and a cover letter containing your full contact information.

Thanks for considering LDP and Ca$h Presents.

Dedications

This book is dedicated to my wife, who is so stomp down on all levels. You're the only true Queen that's fit to sit beside a man like me. I'd splash a hunnit niggaz for you with no hesitation because your loyalty is real, and that's why I keep you spoiled. I love you, Mrs. Jelissa Edwards.

It's also dedicated to our mother in heaven. Mrs. Deborah Lin Edwards. Rest in Peace, Momma. Soon as I touch down in 2019, I'm buying you that grave plot that you deserve.

Rae'Jon and A'Jhani, Daddy crazy about the both of you. I know it's wild having a goon for a father, but we'll figure it out. I got the both of you for life. Soon as y'all old enough to drive, I'm putting you in somethin' foreign. Your bank accounts will stay straight. The future is yours.

To my nephews Aiden and August, uncle TJ will do all that he can to ensure y'all are straight also. I got y'all.

Acknowledgments

I pledge allegiance to the homie, Cash. I'd make them hammers bark for you. Ain't no mafucka was trying to give me and my wife a chance before you stepped in and put that cake up taking a chance on us. For that alone, I'm with you until the end, and I'll face that Reaper with you. My loyalty sealed in blood. All the commas we seeing now is because you took that chance. I ain't never met a nigga that was one hunnit, until you introduced yourself. I'ma keep this pen bleeding for you, and treat it as my hammer so I can make sure that I'm doing my part for the family.

Shawn, you are a true goddess, and it goes further than what you do for the company. You got a crazy ass brother that's coming home in 2019, so them kats out there better beware. You are the truth, my sister, and I appreciate how you hold me and my wife down. Our loyalty for you is sealed in blood, and ain't nothing we won't do for you. Love you, Goddess.

Lastly, to everybody that doubted me, thank you. A hustler needs motivation, and mine came from my own bloodline. Now watch them numbers add up.

Jehovah is real!

T.J. Edwards

Chapter 1

Game bit into his bottom lip and wrapped his forefinger around the trigger squeezing only to find it stuck, locked in place. "Shit!" He looked down on the gun as if it was broken. Then almost immediately his common sense sparked, and he flipped the gun's safety off.

Averie had regained consciousness. No longer fearing for her own safety, but more concerned with the well-being of her son, lying on her back, she managed to kick the gun out of Game's hand. It slid across the floor, and when he turned to dive for it, she quickly got to her feet and jumped on his back, wrapping her arm around his neck, before he flipped her off him.

Boom! Boom! Boom!

Rayjon let out three shots, knocking meat out of Game's shoulder, and watched him fall to his stomach, blood seeping from his wound rapidly.

"Ahhh! Shit! What the fuck?" Game hollered, feeling the pain get the better of him.

Averie ran over and wrapped Jahni protectively in her arms before pushing him under the bed along with herself. She knew more bullets were about to erupt.

Rayjon saw Game moving at a snail's pace toward the gun, as the hole in his shoulder ran like a bloody faucet. "Fuck nigga, you move one mo' inch and I'm bodyin' yo ass. That's my word." He ran over and kicked the gun from Game's reach. He put a knee to his back and aimed at the back of his head with his Mach .90.

Game felt the blood continuing to pour out of him. He felt weak and extremely dizzy. He sighed in defeat as his body went limp. "You ain't gotta kill me, nigga. Just take that bitch and get outta here." He winced in pain and scrunched his face, as he tried to face Rayjon, but Rayjon kept his knee and hand firmly pinned to his back. Rayjon curled his upper lip, "Nall, nigga, my family got plans for you."

***

"Hold that bitch nigga up so my baby can do her thing. She wanna be a part of this family then she gon' have to get down like we get down. No mercy," Ajani said, stepping behind Averie. "Look at this bitch nigga, baby. Just look at this nigga. I want you to think about everything he did to you. Think about everything that he did to our son and I want you to take that shit out on him with this." Ajani handed her a hunting knife that was designed to cut open deer after they had been shot.

Game felt the blood drip from his chin. They held him against the cold concrete wall in his own warehouse. He felt trapped and scared for his life as Averie stepped in front of him with tears in her eyes. He tried to speak but it only caused blood to bubble over his lips. "I'm sss—soorry. Averie, I could have killed you, but I didn't. I gave you a G-pass."

With disregard to his pleas, Game saw her swing forward and the knife pounded into his cheek and crashed into the bone.

"Aaaaaa! Shit! Aaaah! What the fuck?" The stinging intensified as she pulled it away. Then she jammed it into his face again and pulled upward. He started to tap his feet as Rayjon and Ajani held him against the wall. Aiden kept the shotgun pointed at him, while August stood to the side with a big smile on his face.

Averie pulled the knife out of his face prepared to shove it into him again. She felt powerful. She felt that for once, she was stronger than any man that had ever hurt her or took advantage of her femininity. She blanked out and remembered how it felt to have him moving inside of her body.

"Sick son of a bitch!" She stabbed him in the face repeatedly. His blood spurt onto her but she didn't care. She went crazy with the knife slicing, stabbing, poking and only pulling back out when she was satisfied with the bloody mess.

Only then did she drop the knife and fall to her knees in a puddle of her enemy's blood. She looked up at her family and saw how they all looked at her approvingly and very slowly a smile came across her face. She felt she was finally accepted by all of them.

***

"Remember, my brother, the first person I need for you to take care of is a brother of mine that double crossed me. He has over a million dollars in cash of my money. Money that you can have. I simply need his life. Before you settle out East, you need to make a pit stop in Houston. Due to the flood of Hurricane Harvey, it is the perfect distraction. Mail his body parts to the address I gave you and I'll be in touch.

"Remember the money is yours. All I want is his life and every life I have placed on this life. As long as you do things the right way, you will finish a very rich man and have my influence that proceeds the United States." He extended his hand for Greed to shake.

Greed stepped into the man's cell and gave him one of the biggest hugs he had ever given a man outside of his own blood line. "My word is everything. I'll get you home. I owe you my blood. He shook Kabir's hand again looking him in the eye.

***

Rayjon pulled the Range Rover Sport into the prison's parking lot and his mother jumped out looking like an A-list

11

celebrity. He could tell she couldn't even think straight because he couldn't either. His father was coming home, and he knew that meant their money was about to go through the roof and shit was about to get a whole lot bloodier. He couldn't wait. He also couldn't wait to tell him about the bank job that Camryn had set up for him. They would have to buss that move before they left the city.

Ajani sat in his Bentley passing the Loud back and forth between him and Aiden. He couldn't contain himself. His father was finally being released and they were sure to be rich. Rayjon had a bank job in the works, and his son and baby mother were safe.

Ajani still didn't think he could stay away from Stacey, and Averie was screaming she was cool with it. He guessed he'd figure it all out over time. For now, he simply wanted to celebrate his father and by the end of the week, have a few hundred thousand tucked away.

Aiden couldn't wait to go on power moves with his uncle He wanted to prove to the man that he was ready to head his own Ski Mask Cartel.

The whole family gathered into the parking lot as Greed came through the gates. As soon as he got into the parking lot, they all rushed him at once. Before he returned any of their affections he held up his hand, silencing them. "We got a whole lot of work ahead of us and I got some moves in place that's gon' make our family filthy rich. It's just gon' get a whole lot bloodier."

12

Chapter 2

Stanley felt the masked man pull his forefinger back toward his wrist until it snapped, sending a jolt of pain all the way up and down his arm. It hurt so bad that all he could do was scream at the top of his lungs. "Ahhhh! What the fuck is going on?"

Ajani back handed him, knocking out of his office chair. The man fell to the floor, landing on his side. Ajani leaned down and picked him up by his tie.

"Now listen to me, muthafucka, because I'm only gon' say this once. We been followin' yo ass for the last three weeks, clockin' your every move and I know that you got the codes to that bank vault back there. Now if you tell me that you don't, I'm gon' put a bullet in your head, but that's after I snatch up yo daughter and cut her up in front of you.

"So, when I pick you up off this floor, you're going to lead me to that vault back there. It's gon' get cleaned out and then everybody gon' go on their merry way before the manager gets here in approximately thirty minutes. If that bitch show up and we still in here, you gon' regret that shit all around the board, trust me."

Stanley swallowed hard as Ajani yanked him up roughly and threw him on top of his desk. He had a bad feeling in his stomach the whole night prior to that morning. He just felt like something bad was about to happen, but he couldn't fathom what it could be.

Not being able to sleep, he figured he'd get to the bank early, so he could complete the budget break downs that were due in two days. But as soon as he got inside of his truck, he was met by three masked bandits.

As soon as he saw them, his heart skipped a beat. Before he could stop himself, he was pissing his pants. Frozen in place, he carefully weighed his options. *Open the door and run like hell and risk being shot down, or get out the car and play it cool.*

Rayjon stepped forward and sliced him across the face with the blade, trailing it from the bottom of his left eye all the way to his cheek. Then he poked him in the chin. He was accustomed to inflicting pain on his victims right away because it showed them he wasn't to be played with. He had no patience when it came to hitting licks. Everything had to be done immediately being that he liked to keep it moving.

"Get yo bitch ass up and take him to that vault. He got more patience than I do. I'm ready to just kill you and get this shit over with." Rayjon threw him on the floor.

Stanley could feel the blood pouring out of his face. It gushed out of him, and leaked on to his neck. It felt like he was being stung by a million bees at one time. He started to panic and wondered if they were really going to kill him.

He looked up at the men and could only see the ice-cold pupils of their eyes. They looked like death or what he could imagine it looked like.

He put his hands out in front of his face. "Okay, look, I'll open the vault. That's not a problem, just please promise me that you won't kill me after I do. I don't want to die over this money because it doesn't belong to me. I have a family. Two daughters, and a…"

"Son." Ajani finished. "You also have a wife that loves you very much and if you want to make it back to her and your children, then you'll get us what the fuck we want, and we'll be on, our way."

Stanley nodded. He had made up his mind that he was going to give them what was left inside of the vault. It had to be at least two million dollars inside of it. His boss would be pissed but at least the money was insured.

Had they come two days prior, it would have been double that amount. It wasn't their largest bank, simply a chapter of the bigger establishments that spread across California. The one he ran mainly dealt with small business loans.

Aiden reached down and picked him up by the neck with one hand. Stanley kicked his legs and knocked over the laptop that was on top of his desk. It crashed to the floor loudly. "Let's go!"

Rayjon stood back with eyes wide open as he watched Aiden hoist the man over his shoulder and carry him all the way to the vault, slamming him in front of its door, onto his back on the cold hard concrete.

"Open that vault right now. Time is of the essence. He hissed, while his eyes lowered. Aiden hated the man already.

Stanley laid on his back for nearly forty seconds, dizzily. The impact of the ground had knocked the wind out him, making it hard for him to breathe.

Aiden felt like they had spent way too much time on him already. Had it been up to him, he would have brought the man's whole family to the bank and tortured them in front of him until he opened the vault. He knelt down and slashed him across the face three times, causing blood to skeet across the big steel security barrier. "Open it!"

Stanley struggled to get up. Not only did his back feel like it had been crashed into by a car, but his face was bleeding and stinging so bad that he couldn't help crying like a new born baby. The pain was horrible. "I'll do it."

He got to his feet and flipped open the panel, so he could punch in the codes before applying his thumb prints. As soon as he went through the whole procedure, the entire key pad started to flash green and the sound of air being let out of a tire greeted them.

He took the big steel handles and twisted them counter clockwise until the vault popped open.

Aiden grabbed the back of his head and slammed his forehead into the steel frame once, twice and then repeatedly until blood spurt into his eyes and dizziness consumed his body almost immediately.

Stanley's skull made noises as it split further apart from the constant impact. He started to feel sick and then sleepy. His last sights were the evil eyes of Aiden, as the man looked into his face and felt his soul escape. Releasing his body, each man stood directly in front of the vault.

Rayjon pulled the garbage bag out of his waist band and shook it out. "Let's get this muthafuckin' money!" He pulled open the vault's door, with Ajani's help. As soon as they got it open, they ran inside of it with their bags out.

Ajani looked around. To his right there was a pile of money that was neatly stacked. And to his left was the same thing. Directly in front of him was a lot of locked safety deposit boxes. Boxes that he figured would have all types of valuable things. "Damn, Aiden, you kilt dude bitch ass too early. We needed him to open all these muthafuckas," he said, mugging his cousin. He ran to his left and started dumping the stacks of money into his bag.

Aiden was already doing the same thing. "Greed said just the money. All the rest of this shit can be traced, so our only focus is supposed to be the cash. Those were the orders." He growled.

Rayjon shook his head. He hoped they weren't about to get into it. It seemed like every time the three of them went on a move together Ajani and Aiden always wound up getting into some form of an argument. That shit was getting old to him. "Bro, why don't y'all just shut the fuck up and get this money. Aiden, I told you not to kill dude bitch ass. You know Camryn finna go crazy. That's her sister's husband."

Aiden shrugged his shoulders. He really didn't give a fuck.

They should have known that anytime they brought him on a lick that every victim was due to be murdered. He had already made up his mind that he was going to kill Rayjon's girlfriend, along with her sister and kids. Greed had given him that order before they all agreed to go the mission. They were loose ends in his book. Loose ends that he refused to let remain that way. So, before the police even found out about the bank robbery, all of them would be dead. He made that vow to his Uncle Greed.

Ajani had a smile so big under his mask that it was making it rise a little bit. He was already spending the money in his head. They were set to leave California for the state of New Jersey, his homeland, and he couldn't wait to go out there flexing harder than a bodybuilder.

He had a few bitchez in his head that he wanted to stunt on.

Ajani put the last bundle of money in his garbage bag and threw it over his shoulder.

Rayjon was trying to figure out how he was going to tell Camryn that her brother in law had been killed in the middle of the mission. He knew she was going to take it hard.

He wondered if it would make her go to the police. Then decided against it, especially since she had been the one to set the whole thing up. He shook his head. He figured he'd sit her down and just keep shit one hunnit with her. He wasn't with all that lying shit anyway.

Camryn was a big girl. She knew how he got down and

she still chose to let him buss a move on her peoples. So, in his mind, it was her fault.

He'd sit her down and tell her what it was and judge her reaction. If anything looked fishy, he'd have to handle his business. He hoped that he didn't have to. But if he did, he knew that it all was a part of the territory.

"Let's go!" Aiden yelled as he loaded the last of the money into his bag.

***

Greed knocked on the door and adjusted his American Red Cross ball cap. He rolled his head around on his shoulders, trying to loosen up. The air smelled salty and it was humid.

On top of that it was pouring rain. He had water all inside of his knee high black boots. It felt like there was something crawling inside of the right one.

He put his arm against the two-story red bricked mansion and took that boot off, dumping it upside down as the winds of Hurricane Harvey blew across his back.

It wasn't as bad as it had been just three days ago when he had first made it to Houston, and he was thankful for that.

He smacked the boot on its sole, then he dug his hand inside of it and felt around until his fingers came in contact with a huge beetle. He pulled it out and the bug's legs looked as if they were trying to run. He had never seen a beetle that big before. It damn near freaked him out. Before he could take the time out to really focus in on it, the door to the big mansion opened.

Horace saw the huge American Red Cross worker hopping on one leg with his boot upside down and it made him laugh. The workers had been all over the area late last night and whenever he saw one, he felt it was his civic duty to assist them momentarily, by offering his home as a place to rest and to provide them something to eat and drink. He felt it was the least he could do. He opened the door and invited him inside. "Please have a seat. Is there anything that you would like to drink?"

Greed eyed the white man closely. He looked like a skinny version of Jack Nicholson, only redder in the face. Though he was inviting, he carried himself with an obvious arrogance.

Greed could tell right away that he was in some form of law enforcement or had been. Kabir had only told him that the man was an important official that he needed wiped out. He didn't go into any details and Greed didn't force him to reveal any.

An order was an order.

"No thank you. I was just passing by and I wanted to make sure that everybody at this residence was safe and sound. Have you thought about leaving?"

Horace stepped back into the huge living room that was decorated with all kinds of high priced painting.

In the one corner was a grand piano, all white and in the other, a big Harp. The stairs went into a loose spiral and over Greed's shoulder, he could see that the patio led to a massive pool out back. Presently, it was covered with a huge tarp.

"I put six and a half million dollars into this house and made sure that it was designed to withstand any natural disaster known to man. I will never leave it in fear of some storm." He said the last part as if it disgusted him. "Besides it is basically over. There's no need. All the attention is on the one in Florida.

Greed didn't know why exactly, but he didn't like the

white man. He was too cocky. He could only imagine how he was as a prosecutor or whatever his job was.

Out of curiosity, he decided he'd ask him. "Hey, you got yourself a pretty nice house. What do you do for a living?"

Horace smiled briefly and then frowned. "Federal Bureau of Investigations—Anti-Terror Division. He waved his hand through the air. "I can say that I've did alright for myself." He laughed and pointed at Greed. "But you, you're the true hero. Out here braving the elements just to make sure people, like me, are doing okay when I haven't taken one second to think about anybody. Matter of fact, where you're from?"

Greed lowered his eyes and looked the man over closely. "What do you mean where I'm from?" He could feel his heart pounding in his chest. It felt like it was ready to explode. The way the man stared at him like he was nothing was getting the better of him. Horace looked Greed up and down and curled his upper lip as if he were disgusted by his presence.

An all-black German Sheppard casually strolled into the room and stopped by the man's side, looking up at him with its tongue out.

Horace rubbed the dog on its head. "It's not important. Honestly, I just don't care about other people. All of them out there that can't find any shelter or the ones whose houses have washed away because they were too lazy to build it with a solid foundation, screw them all. I don't care about them and I couldn't care any less about what happens to them. I feel just like Joel Osteen. It's just that I have the balls to say how I really feel and he shied away from the truth and chose to hide in darkness. Every man for himself, am I right?" He smiled and clasped his hands together. "Let me get you a beer." He turned and walked toward the kitchen.

As soon as he was out of sight, the dog strolled over to Greed and sat his head on his thigh.

Greed pulled the scalpel out of his sock, slammed it into the animal's belly and ripped downward until the blade came out through the animal's balls. All of its insides fell to the floor and in a huge heap of blood and guts with steam coming out of it. The animal didn't even know what had taken place. It continued to lick at Greed's boots until its heart dropped out of its stomach. Then the animal fell onto its side with its eyes rolled into the back of its head.

When Horace came back into the living room, the first thing he saw was Greed holding his dog up by the neck. All of the animal's insides were hanging out of him.

Horace dropped to his knees and placed his hands on to his cheeks. "Ahhhhh! What the fuck have you done, you sick nigger!" He jumped up and made his way toward his gun case, that was down the hallway and to the right of the living room.

He took off running at full speed with murder on his mind.

Before he could get out of the area, Greed rushed him at full speed after throwing the dog down. As soon as he got to him, he gripped the back of his head into the palm of his hand and with all of his might, slammed Horace's face into the brick wall two feet away from his gun case, splitting his forehead wide open. Blood ran into his eyes, and the impact caused Horace to momentarily black out.

"Nigger that, you racist muthafucka!" Greed picked him all the way up over his head before slamming him down onto his neck, hearing it snap loudly.

All Horace could remember was the man picking him

up into the air before bringing him down at full speed. Struggling to breathe, he tried his best to weaken the grip Greed had on him as he admonished himself for letting a monkey into his home.

Greed picked him all the way up over his head, jumped in the air with him and slammed him down so hard on his neck that he heard it pop. He picked him up again and slammed him with all of his might right on the top of his head. This time a bone popped out of the side of his neck. He picked him up again and dumped him, head first, right on top of his dead dog.

All Horace could remember was the man picking him up the first time and him coming down full speed. Then he felt the impact of the marble floor slamming into his forehead. The bone stabbing out of his neck and the sounds it made while it snapped loudly. Then everything slowly faded to black.

Greed looked down on the man's dead body with his chest heaving up and down. He curled his upper lip.

"Racist muthafucka. How dare you speak ill of my people?" He wondered why Kabir had wanted him murdered so badly. The man had said that he was a part of the Anti-Terrorism Division. He couldn't place the connection, but once again he didn't feel like it was his business to do so.

He had promised Kabir before he left prison that he would knock off the entire list of enemies in exchange for his freedom. That was the deal and he planned on sticking to it.

Greed knew that Kabir was well connected in the political world. The man had pull with the higher up and he knew personally, four other men that Kabir had gotten released from Federal Prison. Greed had heard through the grapevine that Kabir also had enemies in the same political world, enemies that wanted to ensure that he, himself, was never freed.

The game was crazy and Greed didn't understand it.

T.J. Edwards

Chapter 3

Stacey waited until Ajani stepped into the room and she closed the door behind him. Wrapping her arms around his neck, she kissed him on the lips and pumped her pelvis into him.

"I missed you so much, baby. I was worried that something might have happened to you." She looked into his eyes and licked her juicy lips.

Ajani slightly nudged her to the side, and plopped on his bed. "Shorty, I ain't wit all that shit right now. I been up for two days straight trying to get this money right. That lovey dovey shit gotta wait." He laid on his back and exhaled loudly.

Stacey's feelings were hurt. She never liked when he casted her aside. It made her feel unloved and alone.

But she wasn't having that. She wanted him, and she planned on having him. Stacey sank to her knees and started unzipping his pants. She pulled them all the way down to his ankles, then she grabbed his dick aggressively.

She pumped it up and down, while at the same time wetting her mouth with spit.

"I don't care what you talkin' about. You finna let me suck this dick, at least. I been wanting to taste you for the last three days. Now I'm finna make you cum in my mouth and I'm finna play with that shit with my tongue."

Ajani felt it was always room for a little head no matter how he felt in the moment. She guided the fat head into her mouth, wrapping her tongue around it, teasing his pee hole, remembering that he'd told her before he liked when a bitch did that.

Ajani humped into her mouth and lifted his shirt up so his abs could breathe.

There wasn't no secret that his baby mother's little cousin had some good head on her shoulders. It seemed to him that she sucked dick like she was trying to make the grade. She was a beast and only 18 years old, a fresh 18 at that.

He'd been the first one to hit that pussy and ever since he had, she'd been obsessed.

He felt her tugging on his shit with her fat lips and he damn near wanted to moan like a broad.

Stacey sucked up and down his long dick. She held it with two hands and made sure that it was full of spit. She stopped sucking and stroked it up and down with both hands.

"I want you to fuck me right quick before my cousin get home. That bitch be blocking." She popped the dick back into her mouth and sucked strictly on the head. Her tongue ran up and down his pee hole. She popped his dick back out after hearing him moan. "I want you to buss this pussy open. You hear me, nigga?"

Ajani pumped into her mouth and let out a noise that made him want to kill her. He grabbed a hand full of her hair. "Bitch, get yo ass up here and get on all fours. Spread that shit open and wait for me. Now do you hear me?" he asked, gripping her hair even harder.

"Yes, Daddy. I hear you." She felt her juices pouring into her panties. She stood up and slid them down her thighs and pulled her skirt up across her stomach. Jumping onto the bed, she put her face into it, reached behind herself and spread her ass wide open. She could feel her juices running all down her thighs.

Ajani watched the girl spread herself open and he wanted to fuck her until she cried. He stood up and jerked on his long dick, peeping the way her brown pussy lips spread revealing her pink.

Stacey purred. "Omm—shit, Daddy. I love when you play wit my pussy. I'm your lil' girl, so you can do whatever you want to me." She turned her head to the side on the bed and poked her ass up even more.

Ajani took his dick and ran it up and down her pussy, teasing her. His head spreading apart her sex lips, engorging them to the point that they looked angry. He could feel her heat.

When he pulled his dick back, a long string of her juices stuck to his head in a long rope.

Stacey reached under herself and rubbed her clitoris in short circles. "Nigga, if you don't fuck me right now, I'm gon' kill you," she said out of breath. "I swear. I swear on my momma, I'm gon' kill you." Now she was pinching her erect clit, sending jolts through her body. "Fuck me, Daddy! Now!"

Ajani loved when she got to talking that gangsta shit.

He smacked her hard on her ass, and watched it jiggle like brown jello. Then took his fat dick head and placed it at her opening, just in enough to tease her. "Bitch, how you want me to do this shit? Am I fucking for love or am I fucking for blood?"

"Muthafucka, make my shit bleed! I need that dick! Now give it to me!" She spread her ass wide open. "Right now, becau-..."

Ajani slammed forward with all of his might and pulled her into him by her hips. Her pussy was hot and scalding. It felt so good. It tugged at his dick and made him feel emotions he would never admit to.

Every time he fucked her, a part of him fell for her. But he would never let her know that, he felt that would render her all of his power. Not to mention that her older cousin was his baby mother. All he wanted to do was enjoy pussy with no strings, but low key he couldn't deny that she made him feel some type of way.

As soon as his dick sliced through her pussy lips, Stacey screamed at the top of her lungs, especially when she felt him touch the bottom of her stomach. He stretched her wide and it made her feel whole. She felt like a goon was on top of that pussy and the fact that it hurt a lil' bit only added to the pleasure.

"Yes, Daddy! Yes! Ohhh shit! Yes! Please fuck me just like that," she moaned.

Ajani felt her slamming back into him aggressively. He grabbed \her hips and dug his nails into them and really got to banging that shit. He could hear the sounds of her juices and the noise her pussy made as it slurped at his dick hungrily.

"This that shit, lil' momma. Damn, this that shit. Every time I hit this young ass pussy, you be having me say the wrong shit. Every muthafuckin' time!"

Stacey bounced back into him with anger. She was trying to milk him of all of his seed. She couldn't wait to feel those hot globs shoot off into her. It was the best part about fucking him.

"Shit, Daddy, I'm cumming. I'm cumming all over this big ass dickkkkk! Awww shiiit!" She started to shake uncontrollably. Screaming at the top of her lungs for him to fuck her harder.

Ajani felt her walls closing and squeezing his dick. He could smell her pussy in the air and it drove him crazy.

He looked down at the way her ass was jiggling, and he couldn't take it anymore. The heat, the smells, the feel of her womb, the noises she made, it was all too much. He got to fucking her so hard that he was hurting himself. It sounded like he was smacking her on the back again and again, and the headboard was crashing into the wall so loudly it sounded like gun fire back to back.

He felt the pressure building in his nuts and then all at once it was shooting up his dick like a water hose, full of shaving cream.

"Ahhhh! Shit you got that whip! I love this pussy!" He came into her again and again, while she softly squeezed his balls.

She fell on to her stomach with him still lodged deeply within her womb. She could feel his dick pulsing.

"I love this dick, too, Daddy. That's why I'm comin' wit y'all to New Jersey. You gotta holla at Averie 'cause I know she probably ain't gon' want me to come now that she knows about us fuckin'. You got me, right?"

Ajani slowly pulled out of her, kneeled down and started sucking all over her thick ass cheeks and thighs. She was so strapped that he felt like he had to worship her shit.

"I got you, boo. You just let me handle my baby momma. Stay in yo lane. You understand me?" He sucked on her thigh as she laid on her side looking at him, pulling on her nipples.

"Yeah, I guess I can do that. But can you fuck me one more time? You still ain't made me cry yet."

***

"That's one million-seven hundred and fifty thousand right there," Rayjon said, taking the last bundle of money out of the money counting machine. "Shorty told me that we were supposed to get at least three mill. So, we short."

Jersey started to place one stack after the next into one of the two safes. "It's not that bad, baby. This gon' be enough to get us started out east. I already know that your father got some stuff up his sleeves anyway." She couldn't wait until he got back from Houston. He had already gotten in contact with her letting her know that he was on his way home and that the mission was a success. She was ready for him to be back there, so they could pack up and leave California behind. She was worried about the retaliation for Game's murder. He was plugged deeply into the Bloodz, and she felt it was just a matter of time before they clapped back.

She missed New Jersey. She missed her family back home and couldn't wait to see everybody in the physical.

Rayjon shrugged his shoulders. "I just don't want Pops going bananas. He always told me to know exactly how much a lick was gon' bring back before I set it in motion. I told him that this move was gon' bring back at least two million dollars. Now I'm two hundred and fifty thousand dollars short. I'm the oldest so that mean that he watches me very closely. I hate letting him down."

Jersey got up and rubbed her son on the back. "Trust me, your father knows all of these things. He loves you, son, and this isn't going to make him become disappointed in you." She stepped in front of him and took his face in her hands. "It's still nearly two million dollars. What part of that are you missing? Because that's a lot of money, son. I think you've done damn good. I'm proud of you and he will be, too." Jersey kissed him on the cheek and rubbed his back, before bending down to finish loading the safes.

Rayjon loved his mother. She always found a way to put things into perspective. He wanted to run the Camryn situation by her, but he didn't honestly know how to bring it up without seeming heartless. He tried to turn the questioning over in his head a hundred different ways, but none of them seemed right.

Jersey locked the safes in place and stood up. She could tell something was wrong with her son. He was giving off a weird energy. The look on his face told her something was seriously bothering him.

She stood in front of him and grabbed his chin aggressively. "What's the matter with you and don't tell me nothing is wrong because I can read it all over your face. So, spit it out."

Rayjon took a deep breath and exhaled, loudly. "I don't know what to do about Camryn. We had to kill her sister's husband in there and I'm just wondering if it'll be smart to leave this state knowing that she has the knowledge of what took place. Will that put our family in danger?"

Jersey curled her upper lip and then casually smiled. "You know I always liked Camryn. She's a good college girl. She comes from a nice family and on top of that, I can tell that she really loves you a lot. I could definitely see her being my daughter-in-law one day." Jersey shook her head. "It's a shame that she gotta die and you know that," Jersey said, pointing at him with irritation written across her beautiful face.

Rayjon felt like he was ready to choke on his own spit. His heartbeat sped all the way up and all of the sudden he felt like it was way too hot in the room.

A part of him knew he wouldn't be able to keep her alive if anybody had gotten killed during the robbery, which was why he tried to set it up so that a murder didn't take place.

Rayjon simply lowered his head. He really cared about Camryn. He knew she had only set the robbery in motion with the hopes that it would make him finally love her in the way that she loved him. He was sure she never figured it would cost her *her* life.

Jersey frowned and mugged her son with seething anger. "You got a problem with what you gotta do, son?" She looked him over closely for any signs of emotional weaknesses. There was no room for any of that inside of their family. She would never allow for her oldest son to be an anchor to their bloodline. She grabbed a handful of his shirt and pulled him to her. "I asked you a question. Now answer me."

Rayjon looked down into his mother's eyes. "Nall, Momma, I'm good. I was just bugging for a minute. I'm back now. Let's me and you put the rest of pieces of the puzzle together, so we can have a game plan when my father gets back here."

He swallowed his spit and tried not to think about Camryn and the fate that she will eventually have to face.

He tried to not remember all of the good times they'd had together, instead, he tried to remember all of their petty arguments. It was the only way he would be able to release her from his heart and conscious.

Chapter 4

Two days after Stanley's murder, Rayjon found himself in front of Camryn watching her breakdown over the robbery, with his mother's orders playing over and over in his head.

Camryn fell to her knees and covered her face with both hands. "But you told me that nobody would get hurt. You told me that you wouldn't have to kill him if he complied with everything." She fell all the way to the floor with her face planted against it, forehead first. Tears streamed down her cheeks.

Her chest heaved up and down. All she could think about was how her sister had broken down with her arms wrapped around her nieces and nephew. She had never seen her so distraught in her entire life. She felt sick and it was all her fault because she had allowed a man to kill her sister's husband all in the name of receiving his love.

Rayjon crouched down and rubbed her back. He could only imagine how she felt. Apart of him felt sorry for her. He knew she had a lot of weight on her shoulders. He wanted to say some things to comfort her, but he couldn't bring himself to be so fake, knowing that somebody in his family would be killing her soon.

Camryn waited for the words of encouragement and when none came, she reached and knocked his hand away from her. Before standing to her feet, she wiped the tears away from her cheeks.

"You know what, Rayjon? I did all of this because I loved you and I told you I would do anything for you. I've proved myself to you whether you'll admit it or not." She sniffed snot back into her nose. "You freakin' promised me that nobody would get hurt. You said that it would be all about the money and that's it. But now Stanley's dead and it's all my fault. I can't face my sister like this. I don't know what to do and my conscious is gettin' the better of me. I need some time to think or something." She turned around to grab the handle to the door, preparing to leave out of his bedroom.

Rayjon grabbed a handful of her hair and yanked her back to him so that she wound up with her back to his chest. She yelped in pain.

"Camryn listen to me." He hissed into her ear. She could feel the heat of his breath going into her ear canal. "You already know how I get down and I ain't never promised you shit! That bitch ass nigga did too much, and he got his punk ass killed. That ain't yo fault it's his. You already knew what the risks would be, and he crapped out. You gotta woman the fuck up 'cuz you making me real nervous right now and I don't like feeling like I can't trust you. Now can I, or not?" He tightened his grip on her hair.

Camryn swallowed and felt chills go all down her spine. She felt a cool presence step into the room, but couldn't see nobody other than him. She looked into the mirror that sat on top of the dresser and saw the way he had her snatched up and for the first time being with him she started to fear for her life.

She swallowed again and started to imagine her own funeral and she knew without doubt that she had to get out of there. She had to tell Rayjon whatever he wanted to hear if it would insure her safety.

And as soon as she made it out of his house, she would go to the police and tell them everything that happened. She would say that Rayjon made her do it. That she didn't have any choice. Plus, her impeccable record would speak for itself.

"Rayjon, you're hurting me, baby. Please let my hair go I need to face you," she whimpered.

He released her hair and turned her around by her shoulders.

"So, do I have to worry about you?"

She shook her head. "Baby, you already…"

Jersey stepped into the bedroom and jammed the steak knife into Camryn's stomach and pulled it upward ripping open her muscles and tissues along the way. She grabbed her by the throat and led her into the living room. The floors had already been covered with plastic.

"You lil' pretty bitch. I ain't finna let you run that game on my son. I know a stool pigeon when I see one." She pulled the knife out and jammed it back into her again, pulling it upward while she choked on her own blood.

As soon as Camryn saw Jersey come through the door, her eyes got as big as paper plates, especially when she saw her wielding the knife.

Before she could react to what she thought the lady was getting ready to do, Jersey had already slammed the knife into her stomach.

It felt like she was getting poked by a million arrows at one time and then she ripped her stomach open as she pulled the blade upward.

As her insides poured out of her, she felt herself becoming more and more empty and then the pain started. She wanted to scream to tell her to stop but all she could do was vomit her own blood, so much so that it ran down her chin and pooled on to her stomach.

Jersey got her into the middle of the living room and slammed her to the floor aggressively. She looked down on the woman as she pumped her hips into the air, choking on her own blood. It looked like she was trying to gargle a mouth full of tomato sauce unsuccessfully.

Jersey stabbed the knife into her chest trying to locate her heart. Blood spurt across her cheek in the process.

"I'm sorry, lil' girl, but I can't have you ruining my family. Now my son got a thing for you and that's dangerous, so we can't allow for his weaknesses of you to be the reason why our bloodline becomes captive."

Camryn tried to get up, but she couldn't move or breathe.

Her stomach felt like a bunch of cool air was breezing into it. She held her mouth wide open to try and take in oxygen, but the only thing she inhaled was more of her own blood.

Rayjon watched his mother stab his girlfriend again and again. He had already counted forty times and she was still going, all the while mumbling to herself.

He turned his back on the murder scene as the tears dropped down his cheeks. He went into the bathroom to get the bath rub ready for the acid that would eat the flesh from her bones. It was a process that he was all too familiar with.

***

Aiden waited until the last police car pulled away from in front of the Karen's house and then cut a hole into the backdoor's window with his glass cutter.

When the small circular hole fell in, he stuck his hand through the glass and opened the back door just as Tiffany, the youngest daughter, strolled in to get herself a glass of water.

As soon as Tiffany saw the big masked man her eyes got so big that they hurt. She was getting ready to scream, when he lunged forward and picked her up by the neck, squeezing with all of his might with both hands.

She wiggled her feet in the air and tried to hit at his hands in the hopes that he would drop her, but she received no such luck.

Instead, he started to squeeze harder and harder. She began to panic. Her heart thumping in her chest.

The room started to grow gloomy and then her lungs felt like she was choking on a bunch of plastic.

She thought about screaming again, but she was too weak. The world got darker and darker. She imagined her 15th birthday that was not far off and then she faded to black.

Aiden continued to choke her, shaking her lifeless body in the air. Then he backed up into the pantry and lowered her to the floor and kicked her way under the shelf.

He stepped back into the kitchen, after pulling out the deer hunting blade.

He was on his way to the living room when another little girl waltz into the kitchen with tears all over her face. She had probably been crying, mourning her father's death.

She didn't even see him until it was too late. He snatched her by her shirt and sliced her throat four quick times and threw her under the sink where she shook until she bled out holding her neck.

Aiden never felt any emotion for his kills. What was important to him was the job within itself.

He was OCD, he had to complete his tasks in a certain way every time or it would freak him out. He honored his Uncle Greed with everything that he was.

He ordered the hits of Camryn's entire family and that was what Aiden had on his mind every second of every day.

Karen pissed on herself immediately when she saw the big man come through the door of her kitchen with blood all over him. He reminded her of Jason, he even wore a hockey mask, though it was black.

She screamed at the top of her lungs and grabbed her young son, wrapping him in her arms protectively.

"Please don't hurt us! Please! Tiffany, Tamika, run babies! Run right now!" She ordered her dead daughters.

Aiden walked across the small living room and threw the glass table out of the way. It shattered as soon as it hit the floor sending shards of glass all over the place.

Before Karen could get it in her mind to run, Aiden was standing over her. He poked her son in the back with the big blade, then he grabbed him by the back of the head and threw him into the glass china cabinet.

His mother went ballistic screaming at the top of her lungs.

Stanley Jr. felt something poking him into the back that hurt so bad that he started to cry right away. His mommy was holding him, so he knew she would make the pain go away. But then he was up in the air and flying across the room like Superman.

He saw the China Cabinet getting closer and closer until his face crashed into it. Then the glass went into his eyes, his face and his throat. Lastly, his forehead opened up and he fell asleep indefinitely.

Karen tried to jump up from the couch as she saw her son's lifeless body fall to the floor and a pool of blood surround him.

She had to get out of there because she knew she was definitely next. She punched Aiden with all of her might right in the nuts.

He cocked back and punched her straight in the face so hard that it shattered her facial bones. It felt like her whole face was collapsing into itself. He cocked back and punched her again, this time knocking her over the couch.

As she tried to get up, her entire face caved inward. Her skin drooped, and her bones started to fall down her throat. Then she was choking.

Aiden took a plastic bag and placed it over her head. Taking duct tape, he sealed her fate and held her hands until she suffocated.

After she passed away to meet up with her husband and children, he grabbed her by the hair and threw all of her in the pantry, along with the small boy, smiling to himself because he had yet again completed another task for his uncle.

He would be head of his own Ski Mask Cartel yet.

Chapter 5

"The reason why I'm coming to you, Rayjon, is because I don't know what to do. I mean I love your brother and all, but I just feel like he takes me for granted all the time. Fucking my lil' cousin, all in our bed. I mean, come on now. Where does it end?" Averie said, pacing back in forth in the deserted parking lot.

It was two thirty in the morning and she had caught Ajani and Stacey fucking in the bathroom trying to hide from her.

Rayjon watched her pace back in forth, with her hands bent so they rested on the small of her back. He felt sorry for her and couldn't understand why his brother didn't honor her a little more. Averie was a really good and loyal female.

She had held his brother down on numerous occasions when he'd gotten locked down. Rayjon respected her gangsta and honored the way she stood on her biz as a woman. That was hard to find nowadays, he felt.

Averie continued to pace back and forth until he grabbed her arm and pulled her to him. She crashed into his chest. She could smell his cologne and the coconut oil in his hair. He had always made her feel some type of way. A kind of way that she tried so hard to not focus on.

She looked up into his handsome face. "What am I going to do?"

Rayjon leaned down until his forehead was connected to hers. Her heat warming him. He could smell her perfume, and the rawness of her femininity, and it drove him crazy.

His brother had allowed him to hit that pussy one time, and it had been on his mind ever since then. Not just the pussy, but her in general. He felt something for her that he was ashamed to admit and probably never would out loud.

The fact that she was being taken through so much was only adding to his infatuation of her.

"I just want you to know that I got you and I'll never let you fall like that. My brother doing his own thing and he failing to realize how special you truly are, but that's okay because we all got some growing up to do, even me." He kissed her on the forehead.

Averie felt his soft lips touch her forehead and it lit a fire within her. She wrapped her arms around him further, laying into his chest. She could feel his muscles underneath and that drove her crazy.

"Rayjon?"

He leaned back against his Range Rover and hugged her tighter. Looking out into the night's sky, it seemed like it was a million stars decorating it. He was thankful for the gentle breeze. "What's good, Ma?"

"Why you always actin' like you care so much about me when he don't even do that? I ain't nothin' but a lil' bitch from the hood that had his baby. I guess I should be thankful for what I do get from him." She felt like breaking down and crying.

Life was so hard on a black woman, especially after having a kid. Not only was it damaging on the body, but it seemed as if it gave men a reason to take women for granted, she thought.

Before she had Jahni, men were lined up to treat her as a Queen, but after she brought him into the world, it seemed that even her own child's father took her for granted as though she wasn't worth nothing. She was so insecure.

Rayjon kissed her on the forehead again. "Averie, you know you my people. I do care about you and I don't want you thinking that you not worth nothing just because you came from the slums because that's where we from." He held her out in front of him. He rubbed her chin with his thumb. "You are a Queen, baby girl. Don't be letting that shit my brother doing affect who you really are. I know shit ain't right and I ain't gon' sit here and talk down on him for how he gettin' down 'cuz that's not my place. I just want you to know that I really do care about you and I'll do anything for you with no hesitation. Never forget that." He hugged her into him with his eyes closed.

Rayjon meant every word he spoke to her. He thought she was getting the raw end of the deal and he secretly didn't like it. He wanted to protect her and make sure that she was always straight. He knew if she had been his child's mother, he would have died giving her the world.

Averie melted into his body. She couldn't help feeling so secure. It seemed that lately the only time she felt loved was when she was holding her four-year-old son or when Rayjon was around.

Tears began to stream down her cheeks and she couldn't help them from falling. She sniffed snot back into her nose.

"Rayjon, can I ask you something? I mean I need for you to be honest with me, too." She swallowed and wondered if she was going to have enough courage to really ask him the question that had been really dominating her mind as of late.

She hoped it wouldn't run him off.

He wiped her tears away and kissed her on her beautiful cheek. In the moonlight she looked like the perfect black Queen.

"You can ask me anything and you already know I'ma keep shit real as I possibly can." He rubbed her cheeks once again with his thumbs. "Talk to me."

Ever since Averie had been kidnapped, Rayjon had started to look at her differently. She seemed vulnerable to him and in need of his protection. He knew how Ajani was, and he felt that even with all that had taken place, his brother still couldn't tie himself down with one woman. For his little brother, it was money first, then a variety of pussy.

Averie swallowed hard. She was trying to gain enough courage to find out what she needed. She took a deep breath and exhaled loudly. "Okay, I just want you to be honest. You remember how I looked before I had Jahni, right?"

Rayjon nodded his head. "Yeah, I do."

"Okay, forget it. I'm just gon' ask you. Do you think that since I had my son that I'm messed up now? Like do you think that's the reason my baby's father is shitting on me for my lil' cousin?" She broke into a fit of tears. Crying so hard her chest started to heave up and down.

He wrapped her into his embrace and kissed her on the side of the forehead. "Calm down, Averie. Please, man. I hate seeing you like this. This shit ain't cool." Rayjon felt like he was about to shed tears in honor of her. He hated to see her cry, especially for the reason she was doing it. He held her out in front of him and shook her. "Averie, stop this shit, man. You better than this."

"No. I'm. Not." Tears gushed out of her face. She sounded like she was out of breath. "It's not my fault that our son did this to my body. I can't help the way I look now. I try so hard to cover up all these stretch marks." She cried harder.

Rayjon didn't know what she was talking about. To him she had a flawless body. He had seen her naked and paid close attention. Just the thought of her nakedness made him feel some type of way.

"Averie, you fuckin' beautiful girl. What are you talkin' about? You got one of the coldest bodies that I've ever seen. That's on my mother."

She heard the words that came out of his mouth, but her broken heart and shattered self-esteem wouldn't allow for her to believe him. There had been too much damage done. Her being cast aside for her younger cousin was the straw that broke the camel's back. She couldn't help herself from crying harder.

She sank down to the concrete and Rayjon lowered himself with her.

He held up her chin, and made her look him in the eye.

"Yo, I want you for myself even though I know this shit ain't gon' work in the way we want it too. I'm willing to take that chance, though. I wanna spoil you and I wanna show you that you're a Queen. Your body is beautiful to me and I wanna cherish it every chance I get. I ain't saying I'm about to cross my brother, but I'm definitely gon' fill in those blanks that's he leaving open. So, I guess my question to you is, do you wanna fuck wit me on that level? Keep in mind if my family find out, my Pops gon' kill me and my mother gone definitely kill you in cold blood. But I feel like you're worth it. But the decision is yours. So, what do you wanna do?"

Averie felt the shivers go through her. She could not believe Rayjon was willing to step out on the limb for her like that. She was almost afraid to scream that she would take that risk with him in a heartbeat for how it would make her sound.

Then she had to take into consideration what he was saying because they would be flirting with death every single day and every time they laid down together. But it was so hard to not jump out there after being deprived for so long. She needed him in every single way that a woman needed a real man.

"Do you think your family would ever hurt Jahni if they found out we were doing things on the low?" she asked, looking him in the eye.

She knew The Edwards' family was crazy, and they didn't take too well to betrayal and even though she didn't really feel like she was betraying Ajani, she wasn't sure they wouldn't see it that way.

Rayjon shrugged her shoulders. "I don't know what they'd do. I can't really see them hurting him for the mistakes we make, but then again you just never know." Rayjon tried to imagine what them being found out looked like. He didn't think Ajani would allow for anybody to hurt his seed and even if he did, their mother would never permit that to happen.

As much as Averie wanted to be with Rayjon she couldn't imagine risking her son's life for her own selfish reasons. That would have made her a horrible mother, and that she was not. She started to feel her heart breaking all over again.

All she craved was unconditional love. She exhaled. "Rayjon, as much as I wanna be with you right now, I can't take that risk on my son's life. I'm all he really has and vice versa. I wish I would have met you first, though. I don't think I would have been in this position or feeling so lost and unloved. I need you so bad you have no idea how much."

Rayjon pulled her up and looked into her eyes. "Well even so, I just want you to know that I'm here for you and that I care about you." He reached down and cupped her thick behind. Her cheeks felt heavy in his hands. They just felt right to him. "Every chance I get, I just wanna prove to you how sexy this body is and how much you're worth. In my eyes you're perfect, and I'ma hold you down until my last breath. What you think about that?" He rubbed all around her booty, cuffing it off and on.

The way she was popped back on her legs made it open up some for him. He felt himself getting hard right away.

Averie dropped another tear from her eye. She really cared about him and believed every word that came out of his mouth. She felt how he was rubbing all over her and she couldn't help how her body responded to his touch. She wanted him just as bad as he wanted her.

"I believe you, Rayjon, and whatever love you give to me, will make me happy. I just need you. Is that so bad?"

He leaned in and sucked on her neck, biting it a little bit with his teeth. He could smell her perfume and a little sweat and that aroused him. Her body molded against his own.

He pulled her closer to him, so she could feel his pipe pressing against his Gucci's.

"Umm, every time you suck on my neck I get to feeling some type of way," she said out of breath.

The noises he made, while he feasted on her skin, was driving her up the wall. He cuffed her ass and ran his hand into her crease from the back. She could feel his fat dick up against her stomach throbbing.

"Averie, on some real shit. Let me eat this pussy right quick," he said, breathing heavily, sliding his hand into her jeans, in the front.

She had not shaved her kitty in nearly three weeks and she hoped that didn't turn him off.

She spread her legs wider for him as she felt him slip his hand into her panties. He rubbed her pussy lips and squeezed them together, before sliding his middle finger deep into her, while he sucked on her neck.

"I gotta eat this shit. Please, man." Hearing him beg her sent shivers down her spine, making her pussy ooze.

She felt him slide two fingers inside of her and tears escaped her. She leaned her head back and moaned loudly. "Shit! Okay, Rayjon, fuck it. You can eat me, baby. If that's what you really wanna do. If you want, I'll take care of you first." She got ready to drop down in front of him.

In one quick motion, he picked her up and carried her to the hood of his truck and sat her on to it. Stripping her pants down right away.

As soon as they were off of her legs, he ripped her panties from her body and threw them to the ground. He spread her thick thighs and scooted her forward. Her bare ass made a squeaking sound. Then he made her bust that pussy open.

Her brown lips were covered by little black hairs. He could smell her natural womanly scent. She smelled like she hadn't showered in a few hours. Her pheromones shot up his nose and his dick got harder than he ever imagined it being before.

He took his thumbs and spread apart her pussy lips until she exposed her inner pink. "I'm finna show you how sexy you are, I want you to squirt all this shit in my mouth. I need you on my tongue."

She spread her legs wide. He stuck his face between her thighs and slurped her pussy into his mouth as if he was eating raw oysters. He did it loudly as possible and the noise drove her insane. He started to attack her clitoris right away like a mad man. Sucking on her thick lips and licking up and down her center, slurping her juices.

"Uhhhh—yes, baby! Do that shit! Do that shit good just like that."

He trapped her clitty with his lips and ran his tongue in circles around it.

Averie humped into his mouth. She dug her nails into his shoulders and tried to keep from screaming. She was cumming already. Hard. So hard that she could barely breathe.

"Ahh! Ahh! Uhhh—shiiiit! Rayjon, you driving me crazyyy!" Her orgasms ripped through her three at one time, causing her to damn near have a seizure.

She started to move around so much on top of the truck that she almost fell off of it.

Rayjon heard her start to scream and a slight smile came across his face. All he cared about was making her feel better. He wanted to let her know that she was still desirable. That she was beautiful and that he would hold her down to the fullest.

When she got to squirting in his mouth, he tried to swallow it all. Her taste drove him crazy.

T.J. Edwards

Chapter 6

Greed was the last one to sit down. He sat at the head of the table and fixed his napkin inside of his lap. Looking down the long row of faces, he saw his family seated before him.

On the table was the food that Jersey, Averie and Stacey had thrown down on. Baked macaroni and cheese, fried chicken, greens, cabbage, cornbread and for dessert, cherry cheese cake, which was his favorite.

He raised his glass in the air after pouring Strawberry Moet into it. "This is a toast to our new beginnings. This is our family right here. For every person in this room, your loyalty must be worth dying for. Rayjon, Ajani, Aiden, August and even you, Jahni, you are the men of this family and the first line of defense against all predators to our bloodline. You are predators. Nobody sitting at this time shall ever allow themselves to become prey. We are blood. We are royalty. Kings! For each other, there is nothing that we shouldn't do. So, as you sip from your glass, that will be a symbolic gesture of you pledging your loyalties to each other, in blood. Here, here!"

All of the men at the table drank from their glasses one at a time, watching each other very closely. They all knew they were basically saying they were pledging their lives to one another. Any false move and any man at that table could be the one responsible for taking their life.

Greed mugged each man with individual expectation. He loved each one of them but would not hesitate to discipline them to the point of blood in honor of his family.

Nothing or no one was bigger than the body of the family.

He raised his glass again. "To my ladies, Jersey,

Averie, Rachael and, even you, Miss Stacey, you are the arteries in which this body needs to survive and flow smoothly. If you are clogged, then our entire body will die. Your roles are important, because through our women we must gain strength. There is nothing in this world stronger than the black woman. So, to you, I have high standards and will not accept any weaknesses. Your love will remain in this room. You are not to pledge your loyalties to any man or anybody that is not in this room. We are your portion," he ordered. "If you accept these terms of the family, sip from your cup."

One by one, the women drank from their glasses. None more timid than Averie. She had Rayjon going through her veins worse than before. She yearned for him and was having a hard time sitting still without getting antsy over him. She needed him so badly. Just the thought of him made her wet the seat, her panties were soaked. They felt so uncomfortable.

"We leave town tomorrow. Our next stop is back home to New Jersey. There we have a lot of unfinished business. There are men there that tried to get rid of me in more ways than one. Back there is also where my throne has been infiltrated by some imposters. There is a lot of work to be done and we must do it as a family. Everybody must play their roles. That is the only way that we will emerge as Kings and Queens." He smiled. "Give me one year. Just one year and I promise to have a million dollars in each one of your bank accounts, minimum. All I ask for is your loyalty." He looked around at all of the nodding head, then stood up holding his glass in the air. "To family and the road to being filthy rich!"

***

"Averie, can I talk to you for a minute? You know away from everybody else?" Stacey asked, looking over Averie's shoulder at the rest of the family. She prayed that she would permit her at least that.

Averie bounced Jahni up and down on her hip. She really didn't have anything to say to Stacey. In her opinion, the girl had betrayed her and stepped all over her and Ajani's relationship. She felt that if she got her alone that she would try and kill her. "Bitch, what you wanna talk to me about?"

Stacey swallowed the lump in her throat. She didn't want any bad blood between her and her older cousin, especially since she was about to follow her and her baby's father all the way to New Jersey. She felt like she needed to get an understanding before they hit the road.

"Can we take a drive? All I need is ten minutes of your time."

Just as she was about to shoot her down, Ajani came over and grabbed their son out of her arms.

"Y'all go talk. Huh, take my keys, Stacey and y'all be the fuck back here in less than thirty minutes." He kissed her on the cheek and then kissed Averie. Before Ajani could catch himself and realize what he'd done, it was too late. He didn't mean to plant his lips on Stacy in front Averie, in a way to show any signs of disrespect toward her. It was just him being him. That made her flesh crawl.

Once again, she had been his number two instead of one. She looked over at Rayjon as he was hugging his mother, and kissing all over her face, while she tried to get away. She felt a stirring in her heart for him. She wished he could hold her in that moment, or every time Ajani treated her like shit. It was the worst feeling in the entire world. It took all of her willpower not cry right there in front of everybody.

***

Stacey parked the car in front of the lakefront. Looking around she could see a bunch of families out enjoying the summer's sun. They were barbequing, playing volleyball in the sand and some were throwing a Frisbee around. The sun was shining bright, but the wind coming off of the water felt awesome to her.

She let the windows all the way down in the car, and turned down the Dej Loaf's soundtrack.

"Okay, now that you done set the mood and shit, you should be ready to talk. Let's start by you explaining why the fuck you drivin' my baby daddy's car, and not me?" She wanted to reach across the arm rest and smack the shit out of her. Ajani had never let her roll his white Bentley. It was the same car that had almost gotten them killed after Game's spot got hit up for a hefty sum of money. And all of the sudden, Ajani burst on the scene with a brand-new Bentley and a red-faced Rolex.

"Averie, you was standing right there."

"If you didn't want me to drive, you could have told me to hand over the keys. I'm not trying to step on your toes or nothing. You know I love you to death."

"My toes? Bitch, you steppin' all over my life. You literally fuckin' my nigga more than I am. He spends more time with you than he does his own child, or me. So, fuck my toes, that's the least of my worries." She mugged her with hatred. "Why are you following us to Jersey?"

She lowered her head. "I can't be away from him right now," she said it so low that her words were barely heard. She looked defeated and like she was about to throw up.

Averie gave her a look that said she was about to kick

her ass. "What the fuck is you talking about you can't be away from him right now?"

Stacey took a deep breath and slumped back in her seat with her head down. "I'm two months late."

"Bitch, you better be talking about on the rent, because I know you ain't talking about what I think you are." She unbuckled her seat belt.

Stacey still didn't pick her head up or give her any eye contact. She felt sick and was ready for Averie to do whatever she was going to do to her.

"Bitch, you pregnant!" She screamed with tears rolling down her cheeks.

Before she could stop herself, she backhanded her, causing the back of her head to bounce off the headrest and shoot forward, violently. She grabbed her by the hair and yanked her over so that they were forehead to forehead. Blood ran out of the split in Stacey's lip.

Stacey knew it was coming. As soon as her cousin took the seat belt off, she pretty much braced herself for the blow that was sure to come. So, when she felt her hand slam into her mouth and her hair being yanked viciously, she couldn't do nothing but accept the stinging pains that shot all over her from the neck up.

She fought back tears.

"How dare yo ratchet ass get pregnant by my son's father. Bitch, that is your little cousin's daddy. Do you understand what our children are going to be to each other now?" She yanked on her hair even more. "I could kill you!"

Tears rolled down Stacey's cheeks. She felt horrible. Not only did she feel like she had betrayed her family, but she felt trapped, lost and confused. The woman had been there for her ever since she could remember growing up.

Fighting off the bullies at school for her and always giving her a place to lay her head when her mother had way too many men running in and out of the crib that she sold pussy out of. Stacey never had to experience what could have been a tragedy because Averie shielded her from them.

"What were you thinking? Did you stop to think about me or Jahni one time?" She couldn't help crying herself.

Just as she feared Stacey was going to ruin her little family. There was no way around it. She felt like cutting the girl up and getting rid of her body The Edwards' family style.

"I just fell for him, Averie. I didn't know what I was doing. He treats me so good. No man ever has. You know that." She whimpered with snot drooling out of her nose. "I'm so sorry. Just tell me what you want me to do and I'll do it."

Aver knew right away. There was no doubt in her mind what was about to take place, but first she had to find out one thing. "Does he know that you're pregnant?"

Out the window, a group of women strolled over to their car and started to shake their asses right in front of the windshield putting on the best show of their lives. They made sure that their bikinis were all up in their asses. They wanted to give whoever was driving the Bentley the best possible view. All four of them had money on their minds.

Averie let her window down immediately and stuck her head out of it. "Aye! Ain't no men in this car. Ain't nothing but pussy in here and we don't swing like that so y'all can gon' wit that shit." She mugged the girls with hatred.

They acted like they were set on ignoring her. She then punched on the horn, scaring them half to death. They jumped and one little dark-skinned female with tatted paw prints all up and down her thighs turned around and flipped

Averie the bird, before throwing her arms up.

Averie started to open her door immediately before Stacey grabbed her arm, yanking it away. "Don't touch me, bitch!" She went into Ajani's glove box and took the .9 millimeter that was there and slid it in the small of her back like she always seen him do, before jumping out of the car looking for trouble. She was already pissed about what Stacey had told her. She felt like she needed to let off some steam.

Trini saw the caramel skinned girl getting out of the car and she prayed she wanted some drama. It had been a long time since she was able to drop them Compton blows on a bitch and to her Averie looked perfect. She looked way too pretty to be able to do anything harmful. So even though the rest of her college crew scattered toward the beach in fear of the woman getting out of the car, she didn't go no-where.

Averie slammed the car door and walked right up to Trini until she was in her face. "Bitch, you got a problem with me or something?" she asked with her heart thumping in her chest.

Trini frowned. "Who the fuck you calling a bitch? You don't know me like that to be calling me out of my name. I'm from Compton, ho, we can tear this beach up."

Stacey got out of the car in fear of what was going to take place. "Averie, come on let's go. We don't need all this drama, we still have some things to talk about."

Averie turned around with anger written across her face.

"Bitch, get the fuck back in the car right now!" She hollered and watched as Stacey damn near broke her neck trying to get back into it. As soon as she saw her close the door, she turned back to a snickering Trini.

"Seem like you got ho problems. You better off checking that bitch because you ain't got shit coming over here." She looked Averie up and down, challengingly.

Averie smiled, looked back at the car and then fast as lightning swung and punched Trini so hard that she fell backward until her head hit the concrete. She never saw the blow coming.

As soon as the woman fell out flat on her back, Averie straddled her and pulled her up by her weave. Blood gushed from her nose and ran down the sides of her cheeks.

"Bitch, next time somebody tell you to get the fuck away from their car, you listen. And shit like this won't happen." She stood up and looked around.

The woman was actually snoring loudly under her. The three women that she had been with watched from a safe distance with their eyes wide open. She had the attention of nearly everybody on the beach. They had their phones out recording her.

Before Averie got back into the car, she closed her eyes, took a deep breath and tried to calm herself down. She got back into the Bentley and put her seat belt around her, then replaced the gun. "Bitch, I asked you if he know you pregnant already or not?"

Stacey was shaking so bad that it looked like she was outside naked in the freezing cold. She was terrified of her big cousin. She didn't even know she'd got down like that, and instantly she started regretting everything that had taken place between her and Ajani. She didn't want her to fuck her up like she had done the woman on the beach. She didn't know what to say.

"Answer me!"

She damn near jumped out of the car and ran. "Yeah. He knows. He been knowing for three days now."

"And what he say? Do he want y'all to keep it or not?"

She took a deep breath and braced herself for what she was about to say.

Stacey lowered her head. "He said that he was happy, but I had to tell you on my own."

Averie blinked tears. She felt like she was ready to throw up. It seemed that Ajani was dead set on replacing her with somebody younger. Somebody from her own bloodline. She was hurt, and felt sick to her stomach.

Stacey was crying real tears now as she drove away. "Say something to me, Averie. If you want me to drive somewhere so you can kick my ass, I'm okay with that. I know that I deserve it, and I won't even fight back."

Averie curled her upper lip as her life flashed before her.

She had visions of taking Ajani's gun and blowing her little cousin's brains all over the windshield. Then she would drive back to his house and body him, too. But she couldn't. She didn't think she could live in a world where he wasn't hers or he was taking care of another woman's baby, even if it was her little cousin.

She felt that their own son suffered enough neglect from him. Now he would be forced to share his father with a whole other baby. That wasn't fair.

"You know what, Stacey, I wish you the best. I just wanna let you know that after you have that baby and you get all them stretch marks and shit or your pussy open up a little more, that he gon' kick yo ass to the curb and find somebody younger than you because he likes young pussy. You were hot because you were young and fresh. After you have that kid, you ain't gon' be shit. That I can assure you."

Averie made that assumption from her own experiences with Ajani. Why would her own cousin be any different? No matter what Averie was saying to her, she just couldn't believe he would ever do her like that. He had said he loved her and she believed him with every fiber of her being. Nobody was going to change her mind, because she loved him, too.

Chapter 7
Newark, New Jersey

"Pops, we ain't even been here a full day and we already on business. I'm so glad you back home," Ajani said, sliding the mask down his face, before slamming the big magazine into the AR .33 assault rifle.

He had a hundred and fifty shots, a vest protecting his chest, and a crazy ass old man that was two times as vicious as he was.

Since they had been gone, his father had gotten word that one of his old stomping buddies was set to testify against him when the secret indictment came down. Had all of that not been ceased, Mack would have taken the stand and made sure they buried Greed six feet under the prison grounds.

Greed never took too lightly to disloyalty. He felt like it was a sin punishable by death.

"Son, it's been a while since I got down with you, but I'm finna show you how to treat an enemy that you hate. It's *no mercy* season." Then he looked to everyone. "Y'all got that?"

Aiden, Rayjon, August, and Ajani all nodded in unison.

***

Mack walked around the living room, watching his workers closely, as they chopped through the kilos of rock cocaine before placing small portions on a scale to make sure they were bagging the right amounts of grams.

He had the air conditioner all the way up to keep them awake. Fifty kilos was the mission. They had been bagging dope for the last three days and he hoped that by the end of the day they would be finished and ready to open up shop once again.

For him, it was all about the money. He lived, ate and shitted out money. That dope boy shit had been in him ever since he was nine years old, selling weed for his uncle.

"That's what the fuck I like to see. Everybody working together. One chops and weighs. The other bags and tie. This is what success look like. All of you muthafuckas are eating. Every last one of you because of me. Let me run the show and you'll never starve." He hollered, looking over his workers as they sat at the two picnic tables that had been pushed together the long way.

They had a nice system going, but quiet as kept, none of them could wait to be done. He had not allowed for them to go home in nearly five days. Whenever there was a big shipment coming in, he expected for them to stay at his hip. They couldn't leave the trap for any reason. Those were the rules. If they broke them, they paid severe consequences.

"Keep this shit up and the trap will be back open this afternoon." He nodded and took a cigarette from behind his ear, lighting it and inhaling deeply, before exhaling.

Bong. Tink, tink, tink, tink. Shhhhhhhhsssh!

The smoke bomb exploded after crashing through the window. A thick cloud formed in the building. It was so thick that nobody could see in front of them.

Bong. Tink, tink, tink, tink. Shhhhhhhhsssh!

Another crashed through and went off.

Mack felt like he was about to have a heart attack and so did everybody else. He could hear them murmuring and it sounded like they were starting to panic.

Boom! Boom! Whoom!

The front door flew off of its hinges and slammed against the wall, then all of the lights went out and all Mack could see were blue beams, before the gun fire erupted. He fell to his stomach and put his hands over his head.

The first thing Ajani saw after he kicked in the door was a fat nigga with a black wife beater on that was stretched out.

Boo-wa! Chit-chit. Boo-wa!

The bullets knocked two huge holes through him. The first bullet knocked the meat out of his neck and the second blew half of his head off. Ajani smiled under the mask. He loved Shotguns. They always did half of the work for every mission.

The big man fell into a clump of bones. Ajani stepped over him and ran into the trap with the shotgun pressed firm against his shoulder in firing mode.

The man never got a chance to duck for cover. As soon as the door was kicked in, he went to reach for his gun but fell short of it as he heard and felt the shotgun blast.

The fire spit from the barrel and the bullet slammed into his chest. It felt like he was having the worst asthma attack in the world. The shot knocked him against the wall and the last thing he saw was one part of his face falling one way and the other side, another.

Rayjon crept through the backdoor after Aiden cut the power.

He slowly made his way up the steps. Aiden kicked in the door that led to the downstairs of the duplex. As it flew open, two shots came their way, one smacking Rayjon in the chest and knocking him backward. He flew against the wall as if he had been picked up and thrown by a big ass wrestler. His chest felt like somebody was digging in it with a screw driver. "Fuck! I'm hit." He got dizzy and started to fade out.

Aiden saw this, and his eyes got bucked and then very low.

He looked into the door where the shots had come from and got angry. He waited until he heard three more shots and then he dropped to the ground and slid on his belly into the house.

Smoke invaded the entire crib. It was heavy, with nearly no visibility.

The first thing he saw was a man hiding on the side of the refrigerator, he looked to be loading his gun. Aiden aimed, and bussed.

Boo-wa!

The man saw the spark in the kitchen and the next thing he knew it felt like he had a horrible migraine headache. Then there was blood everywhere and he couldn't stop himself from falling forward. He heard another shot, and everything faded to black.

Aiden slid over to the man whose head he had just knocked off of its' shoulders. His brains had splattered through his face.

He took the gun off of the floor and put it on his hip. Continuing to low crawl on his stomach. He saw a man kneeling down looking like he was trying to find a way to escape. In the front of the house, he could hear the sounds of rapid and automatic gun fire. It sounded like the fourth of July. He aimed his banger at the potential refugee and bussed.

Boo-wa!

He watched his head snap back violently and then he fell on his face.

After insuring that the kitchen was clear, Aiden went back into the hallway and snatched up Rayjon.

It didn't take long for the shots to stop. Greed had the rest of the trap all laid out on their stomachs at his mercy, just like he liked it.

Ajani finished duct taping Mack and drug him to the back of the house and out of the door, loading him into the trunk of the car.

Greed knelt down on one knee. "It's fucked up y'all gotta die because you chose to follow this rat ass fuck-nigga, but that's how the game go. If you'll follow a rat, then you'll eventually turn into one." He shook his head and gave August the nod.

The young killer knelt down and went down the line slicing one victim's neck at a time. He pulled their hair roughly and exposed their neck. Sawing into them in a frenzy. He loved it, the feel of a hot body becoming a corpse all at his hands.

John-John felt the blade touch his neck and then it ripped it open. He felt his Adam's apple fall out.

Mickey felt the man yank him by the dreads and then the ridges sawing into his neck. His blood spurting onto his chest looked like hot coffee. He started to cry but before a tear could drop, he was dead.

All down the line it was more of the same. Before it was all said and done, August had murdered nine men, by the blade.

Greed looked on with approval. To him there was nothing like having looney killers around him that honored his position. He felt powerful. He felt like his family was on the right track. Now he had to personally make Mack pay for his sins.

***

"Pull on that chain, son." He ordered Ajani.

He tightened his gloves on his hand and watched as Mack was hoisted all the way into the air, hanging upside down. He knelt down and looked over his tool box, trying to decide which utensil he was about to use on the snitch-nigga.

Ajani lowered him just enough so his father could reach him. After he was at the right height, he tied the excess chain around the big bolt that poked out of the brick wall in the warehouse. He looked over his shoulder and saw that Rayjon was eating a big bag of Doritos, crunching loudly. Aiden looked on unamused, while August rubbed his hands together in obvious excitement.

They were inside of an abandoned steel plant. All around them was trash and dope fiend's paraphernalia. It smelled like shit and piss. The air was muggy and there was barely any light inside of it. The only light that came through shone from the window. The moon illuminated the plant as much as it possibly could.

Rayjon threw the match inside of the garbage can and set the paper on fire. The fire's light helped them to see better.

Though his chest was still killing him, he felt so happy to be alive. He silently praised his mother for her role. She had basically made him put on a bullet proof vest. Had she not did that he would have probably been dead.

He popped another Dorito into his mouth and watched the scene unfold in front of him.

Greed stepped to the hanging Mack and punched him with all of his might right in the mouth. Before he allowed the man to get used to that punch, he hit him with a flurry of six more.

Hitting all across his face, shattering his bones, he finally stopped. When he was done, blood dripped out of the man's mouth in long, thick ropes. He noted that he'd knocked out his entire front grill.

Mack hung upside down and didn't know what to do.

His face hurt so bad that he was already crying. He ran his tongue across his upper row of teeth and felt they were missing. All of his blood had rushed to his head and what didn't was dripping out of his mouth.

"Why the fuck you doin' this, Greed?" he asked out of breath.

He didn't know why the man was targeting him or how he had gotten out of jail. The feds had assured him that he would have never seen the light of day again. And even after they had told him all of this information, he'd still refused to rollover on him.

Greed curled his upper lip, stepped forward and grabbed Mack's swinging head. "You rat muthafucka. After all the shit I done for you, you choose to fuck with them Alphabet Boys over me?" He pushed him away so that he'd swing on the chain. Then he punched him right in the left eye so hard that it shattered the socket. The whole left side of his face swelled immediately.

"Aaaahhh! You fuck-nigga! I ain't never been no snitch. Somebody sending you off, kid. You know how I get down!" he said, feeling his head swell. The pain was unbearable. Every part of him was stinging from the shoulders on up.

"I'm the muthafucka that fed yo whole family while you was serving a bid. Five fucking years, nigga! Five years and they ain't never want for shit! You owe me more loyalty." He walked up to him and took the vice grips and clamped them on to his cheeks, tightening the grip as much as he could while Mack screamed at the top of his lungs.

His cheeks felt like it was being stabbed into by the biggest wasp in the world. The more he screamed the tighter it seemed that Greed gripped his flesh.

Greed saw the skin coming away from the bone of

Mack's cheek and he loved the sight of it.

Aiden heard Mack screaming and saw the way his skin was being ripped from his face and he became excited. He wished he could help. He had never thought about the vice grip move but it was definitely something he would be adding to his arsenal.

"You ripping—off—my—ahhh! Greedd! Ahhh! Fuckkk!"

Greed dropped the piece of cheek into his hand and threw it to Rayjon. "Pass that shit around because that's what disloyalty look like."

Rayjon swallowed and turned the man's discarded cheek over in his gloved hand. The first person he thought about was Averie.

He prayed it never came to that for them. He knew his father would never hesitate to discipline him in that fashion.

Greed got to pulling off another part of Mack's cheek. He held it in the air.

Mack had been his stomping buddy since day one. He never imagined he'd be the one killing him one day. But that was just how the game went.

He swallowed and handed that huge piece of cheek to Rayjon. "Loyalty, son! That's what our bloodline breathes on. If you take the loyalty out of our family, then all we got is death." He stood back and pulled out an ice pick.

He gulped one last time as all of the memories of laying niggas down with Mack came across his mind's eye.

As teens, they had been souljahs. Fearing no man. Bussing their guns back to back at their enemies with no heart.

Mack had saved his life more than once. While Greed served a five-year bid, Mack held him down, and never tried to fuck his baby mother one time, even though she threw the pussy at him on a regular. One time, he even had to pull out a belt and whoop her ass to keep her in line. Long as he was roaming the streets and his man's wasn't, she wasn't allowed to fuck nobody.

Mack felt like scalding hot water was being poured on to his face. The pain was excruciating. He had never felt anything like it before. He thought about his new born daughter and then her mother. He wished he could kiss them one more time.

He saw the big flabs of his face being passed around and it almost made him want to pass out.

Ajani stepped forward and held up a mirror, so he could see himself. He looked like he had been attacked by a lion. Large pieces of his skin, missing.

Ajani shook his head and then took the salt and poured it all over him then jumped back to see what Mack would do. He was accustomed to men going crazy and screaming at the top of their lungs before becoming hysterical.

"Ahhhh! Ahhhh! I can't take this shit no more! Kill me right the fuck now. Please! Please, Greed. Man, I'm begging you. Don't do me like this."

Greed looked back at his family and gripped the ice pick tighter in his hand. "Tell me something to end your torture. Anything, nigga. Save yourself."

The salt was stinging him. It felt like acid was being poured into his face. He pissed all over himself and then his bowels released. Hot smoke came from his ass.

"Envy. Envy. Your brother, Envy, didn't want you back out east, kid. That nigga silently hates you 'cuz of your wife. He gon' body you when it's all said and done. Mark my words, sun. He fucked with them Feds, too. I ain't talk, but that nigga did. Now kill me!"

Greed looked over his shoulders and nodded at his

bloodline.

Turning back to Mack, he took the ice pick and proceeded to stab him in the face over two hundred times. His face looked like smashed Raviolis.

Chapter 8

Averie ran and jumped in the car. As soon as she was inside, she told Rayjon to step on the gas and he gave her a look that told her she was acting like she was out of her mind.

He slowly started up the truck and threw it in drive.

"Just chill. I told Ajani I was gon' take you out to get your hair done and he was cool wit it. I guess he wanna spend some time with Stacey anyway because they got some shit they need to work out."

As soon as Averie heard that, her heart sank. She felt like shit. She wanted to throw up, but she had already promised herself she wasn't about to let him ruin her. She felt she needed to be strong, and emotionally move on. She couldn't help lowering her head, though.

Rayjon reached over and rubbed her soft chin. "You okay, lil' momma?" He eyed her from the side of his face and tried his best to keep his eyes on the road.

He knew she was hurting, so he'd decided he was going to do all that he could to take her out and show her a good time. Every female needed pampering, but due to the fact that she was a hardworking mother that meant she deserved it.

Averie exhaled. "I guess I need to get over him because if I don't, then he gon' wind up killing me. I'm not strong enough to handle these feelings that are being stepped on. I just want to be loved. That's all I ask." She felt the tears fall down her cheeks.

Rayjon pulled up at a red light and leaned over and pulled her into his embrace. Hugging her before tilting her chin up and kissing her on her full lips. They sucked on each other for what felt like five whole minutes until the cars behind them started blowing their horns.

They broke their kiss, both breathing hard and duly aroused.

Averie's chest was heaving up and down. Both of her nipples were so hard they hurt. "Every time you kiss me, Rayjon, you be having me feeling some type of way. That shit gon' be so dangerous if I start to fall in love with you right after being in love with Ajani. I'm so confused right now.

Rayjon could feel his heart beating just as fast. I don't want you falling in love with me, Averie. I just wanna make sure you're good at all times. I know you got it hard, and I know you handling business for my nephew. I would be less than a man if I didn't find a way to hold you down in some way. I just want to make you happy as much as I possibly can. I got you, and I ain't never gon' drop you. That's my word."

Averie felt her lips quivering, and she couldn't help crying into her hands. Nobody had ever taken an interest in her. The only thing they'd ever cared about was her body. After they got what they wanted, she was always kicked to the curb, even if she had only given them a little head.

For Rayjon to be in the streets, and trying to console her in the manner that he was *was* blowing her mind.

As he let down the windows in his Range Rover, she could feel the cool air blowing across her face and it felt so damn good.

"I can't promise that I won't fall in love with you, Rayjon, but I will try not to. For now, whatever you give me, I will appreciate."

Rayjon threw a bundle of hundred dollar bills on to her lap. "That's fifteen bands right there. We finna spend all of that on you. Whatever you want, however much you want,

that shit is all on me because you my Queen for the day."
He grabbed her by the hair and pulled her to him until they
locked lips.

***

Ajani walked up to his Aunt and hugged her like he
hadn't seen her in over fifty years. The short red bone
woman felt his muscles wrap around her, before picking
her up off the ground.

"Boy, you better put me down before I scream," she
teased.

She looked around and saw all of her dancers that were
presently in the club looking at her with eyes wide open.
They didn't know who the fine brother was that had her in
the air.

What they peeped was the fact that he pulled up in a
2018 Bentley and rocked a red-faced Rolex on one wrist,
with a diamond-frozen bracelet on the other. He looked like
money, smelled like money and all of them was seeing
baby daddy potential.

He lowered her to her feet and scanned the dressing
room.

He saw so many thick bitchez in it that he couldn't keep
his mouth closed. There were red bones, caramel skinned
chicks that were more strapped than Batman. Some of them
had thighs so thick that he wanted to run over and just bite
their asses that were poked out of G-strings.

His dick got hard immediately.

Vanity grabbed his hand and pulled him out of there.
"Let's go, baby, before you get me in trouble." She pushed
him out of the dressing room. "And to all you bitchez,
hands off. That's my muthafuckin' nephew. If I catch anyone of you hoez trying to run that shit on him that I taught

you, we gon' have a problem. I ain't playing either."

More than one of them rolled their eyes, or sucked their teeth loudly. None of them really believed he was her nephew. Majority thought he was a young nigga that she was fucking and was probably going to be coming around a lot, so she couldn't handle the competition. Typical shit in the stripping life.

Vanity closed the door to her office and looked him up and down. She had to admit he had gotten fine. She saw right away why the bitchez was staring at him the way that they were.

"Boy, what brings you to my club all out the blue?" She stepped around the desk and sat in the big leather seat.

Her office was cozy. It wasn't too big or small. It had two big windows inside of it that overlooked the main stages. She had the blinds rolled up, so they could look down at everything. An all pink Lenovo 15-inch laptop decorated her desk along with a few other girly things.

Ajani saw that big ass booty poking out of her tight Gucci dress and the way it conformed to her hips. The top of the halter dress nearly exposed all of her yellow titties. He could make out the big brown nipples easily. He felt his dick rise to attention.

Vanity had always drove him crazy ever since he was a little kid and he and Rayjon used to sneak in her closet and watch her get dressed. She had the best body he had ever seen on a woman and still did. His obsession with her had not gone anywhere. "I see you still bad as hell, TT."

"And I'm still your aunt, so you better focus in on something besides my ass."

"What about them pretty ass titties?" He licked his lips. She rolled her eyes. "Boy, what can I do for you?" She threw her long hair over her shoulders and batted her eye-lashes at him.

Ajani pulled out twenty thousand dollars in all hundreds.

He held them in two hands. "On some real shit I want a lap dance. I want that fat ass booty in my lap and I'm willing to pay for that shit. I ain't playing either." He was dead serious. He didn't give a fuck if she was his father's youngest sister or not. He wanted her all over him.

Vanity licked her tongue across her lips and smiled. She couldn't believe how he was coming at her.

For as long as she could remember, he had always been a pervert and the look on his face told her he was dead serious.

"Boy, if you don't put them lil' chips back up and get out of my office before I have security come in here and throw yo ass out. You gon'…"

Ajani dropped all of the money all over her desk and pulled out his pistol, after closing the blinds in her office. "Anyone of them niggas roll up in here, I'm gon' let all seventeen ride in they ass. You know I don't play that shit. I want what I want, and I want that ass in my lap right now. So, what's good?"

Vanity stood up and came around her desk, stopping directly in front of him. She looked up and into his eyes. "You better put that pistol up and have some respect for my establishment. You know that shit don't scare me."

He smiled, and put the pistol in the small of his back.

"I ain't trying to kill no nigga today. I been back in town for like three days and the only person I been thinking about is you. I ain't no kid no more, so all that babysitting shit that you used to do to me when I was little, I didn't know what to do back then, but I do now, and I ain't leaving this office until you give me that lap dance." He pulled her close to him and pulled up her short skirt, palming her fat ass cheeks before carrying her to her desk top and swiping everything on the floor.

Vanity felt jolts go all through her body, she couldn't believe that he remembered all of that shit.

***

"You sure that ain't too much?" Averie asked as she brought all of the bags to the front of the register, and saw the amount owed. It was well over six thousand dollars and she started to panic.

Rayjon licked his thumb and started to peel off hundred after hundred-dollar bill. Even though he'd just given her a bundle of cash, he still felt like spoiling her a little more. The price wasn't nothing. All he cared about was making her happy and the look on her face was payment enough.

"Yo, like I told you before, I got you. So, don't worry about nothing. Today is your day, and we celebrating you."

She wanted to run over and wrap her arms around his neck.

He had already gotten her hair, nails and toes done, and bought her some Sephora products. And after all of that, she had gotten a massage and seaweed wrap. She felt loose and so much like a lady. She didn't care what she had to do before they headed back to the family, she was going to make it her business to give him some pussy. He more than deserved it.

***

Vanity bent all the way over and twirled her hips in a slow circle while Ajani rubbed her back and slid his hands down, so they were squeezing her thick thighs.

He had her skirt pulled all the way up and her panties were at her feet, wrapped around her right ankle. He could smell her pussy in the air along with the scent of Chanel No.5. All of it had his dick harder than a gang banger. The heat coming from her crotch was searing his lap. He squeezed her titties and massaged them.

She moaned and laid her head back on his shoulder.

"Damn! You got me on this taboo shit. I don't even get down like this, boy." She felt him lowering her shoulder straps. Her breasts hung on her chest. Both nipples heavily engorged. The forbidden aspect of it all was driving her crazy. She could feel his hard dick under her ass. She ground harder into it.

He grabbed her waist and humped into her as she sped up the pace.

Sza's hit song *The Weekend* was playing in the background, and he could feel her jerking his dick back and forth. He was doing everything he could to not cum in his pants. Things got so intense he moved her off of him.

Vanity opened her eyes as she felt herself being lifted off his lap. She was seconds away from getting off herself. She didn't know what the problem was. She turned around and saw him lowering his Tom Ford jeans. His dick sprung up like a huge brown baseball bat, heavily veined and throbbing.

He pumped his dick back and forth. "Bend yo ass over that desk right quick. Hurry up." He sounded as if he were out of breath.

Suddenly she snapped out of it. *I can't do this,* she thought.

I ain't finna fuck my brother's son. What type of shit is that?" She started to pull down her skirt. "Ajani, we gotta stop this shit. You got yo lap dance and I shouldn't have even done that. Now pick up that money and go, boy."

Ajani looked at her like she was crazy. She had to have lost her mind. He saw the way her nipples were poking through her Gucci top. Juices ran down her thighs and traveled along her ankles. She was just as hot as he was.

"Vanity, you finna give me some of that body. I ain't playing either." He stepped toward her and she stepped backward.

Holding her hands in front of her. "Baby, it's time for you to leave. We done went far enough. I love you as my nephew and that's..."

Ajani picked her up and she automatically wrapped her legs around him. He fell to the floor between her legs. Her hot pussy all up against his stomach. He snuck his hand between them and rubbed over her juicy pussy lips. They were covered in a gel like fluid. He pushed her knees to her chest, making her buss her kitty wide open.

As soon as Vanity felt his mouth cover her sex she came right away.

"Uhhhh! Sheeeiiit!" She was shaking uncontrollably.

His tongue went as far into her as it could. She felt his lips wrap around her clit, then he was sucking for dear life. She came again, looking like she was having a seizure.

Ajani saw the way her thighs were jiggling as she shook, and it drove him crazy. He pulled down the straps of her top, exposing her brown titties, pulling on the nipples causing her to scream and shake even harder.

He flipped her over on to her stomach, spread her ass cheeks and licked in between them. The salty taste, coupled with the scent of her sweat drove him crazy.

Vanity struggled to get up. She couldn't allow for him to put his dick into her body. That would be taking things way too far. She tried to scramble and get to her feet.

Ajani tackled her back to the floor. She fell on her stomach. Her legs cocked wide open, pussy exposed. He climbed on to her bac, and spread them further. Taking his dick, he rubbed it up and down her slimy slit. Her juices coated his head immediately. He started to force the head inside of her, watching her lips spread.

"Please don't do this, nephew. Don't do me like this, baby. We are family." She looked over her shoulder at him pleadingly.

Ajani's heart was beating too fast. He had to have a piece of that pussy. To him there was no way around it. He grabbed a handful of her curly hair and pulled her up to all fours.

Her ass crashed into his lap, after she yelped from having her hair pulled. Taking his dick, he put the head to her entrance and pushed her face to the floor. "Beg me for this dick!"

Vanity felt the juices pouring out of her. Her clit was throbbing and vibrating like someone was ringing a line. Her walls squeezed together. She felt him smack her on the ass and it nearly made her cum.

"Shit! Don't do this." She whimpered, jerking her head away from him. She tried to get up, but he pulled her back down.

Ajani sucked his middle finger and slipped it into her ass, feeling it pull at him. "Beg me for this dick, Vanity, I ain't gon' tell you no more." He growled, smacking her on the ass again.

Vanity moaned. Defeated and ready to be filled, she reached behind herself and spread her ass cheeks wide.

"Fuck this pussy, then, and I mean you better fuck me hard. If you put yo dick in me and you don't kill my shit I'm gon' tell your father that you raped me. You better tear this shit up. Now go!"

She stuck her face in the floor.

Ajani forced his dick head into her and then slammed forward with all of his might. She yelped, and her heat swallowed him. He gripped her hips and started to fuck her like he hated her guts. It didn't take long for the tears to leave her eyes. Before it was all said and done they wound up fucking for three hours straight and ended with the taste of each other on their tongues.

***

"Rayjon, before I go back into this hotel, I just wanna let you know that I appreciate everything you did for me today. I have never felt more special. I know you didn't have to do anything that you did, but I am thankful just the same." She lowered her head.

He picked her chin up with his fingers. "I ain't gon' keep telling you that you gotta keep this head up. You're a Queen, and I'm gon' forever hold you down. Long as I got it, you got it, like my Pops said, *you women play a crucial role inside of this family, too.* The last thing we need is for y'all to be out there depending on other niggas. Fuck that. I ain't gonna, especially when it comes to you. I'll be yo duck off. Ain't no nigga finna be playing wit yo head and shit." He frowned.

Averie tried to fight back the tears. She was falling for him already and it was so hard for her to not melt into a pool of flesh and bones. She reached over and gripped his thigh.

"I already know that nothing comes free in this world. Everything that a person wants they have to fight for it, or pay in some way. So at least let me suck yo dick, Rayjon, that way I don't feel like you did all of this for me and I didn't do anything for you." She reached for his zipper.

He moved her hand out of the way and pulled her to him, hugging her with love. He felt a deep compassion for her and could tell she was lost.

He knew the life that she'd lived, knew that nobody had truly took the time out to really love her in the way they were supposed to. For that reason, she became a weakness to him that was extremely dangerous.

"Averie, you ain't gotta do that shit. Everything I did today is because I feel like you deserved it. I care about you. If I gotta tell you that over and over again, I will." He kissed her on the forehead as tears flowed down her cheeks.

Chapter 9

Errrr-uh!

Greed slammed on the brakes and nearly smashed his Benz truck into the all-black Hummer that appeared to drive at him head on.

He had the right away on the one-way street. His senses told him that there was going to be trouble. He grabbed the mini Mack from under his seat and cocked it back. Doing the same to the .40 Glock that had a clip in it that shot 120 times. It looked like a Pez dispenser hanging from the handle.

Out the window, the Hummer's doors opened up and five men jumped out with AK47's in their hands. Their faces were covered half way with black rags.

Four all black Ducati's pulled up alongside of his truck.

The men that drove them got off of their bikes and pointed their weapons at his driver side window. It looked like he was surrounded on all sides. His heart got to pounding in his chest. He dug his hand all the way into the bottom of his seat and pulled out one of the grenades that he'd had hidden. He figured that if he was going to go out, then he was going out like a muthafucking gangsta.

He was the chief of the Infamous *Ski Mask Cartel.* There was no way in hell he wasn't gon' make a statement. He pulled the pin out of it and got ready to roll down his window.

The first thing he thought about doing was rolling the grenade under the hummer and blowing that bitch all the way up, then he would spit every bullet he had in an attempt to get away. Soon as he made his mind up and hit the picture on his dashboard that had Jersey's face lit up, it called her immediately and she picked up.

"Baby, I'm cornered. It's a wrap for me. Make sure you raise my sons to be men. August and Aiden the same. Protect our bloodline and keep it pure. I love you, and you got all of the Swiss accounts info. Live good."

"Baby, wait…"

He ended the call and took his thumb off of the lever for the grenade to detonate. He started to count up to five. He knew it would explode on the eighth second. He kept his eyes on the big Hummer and tried to not think about his family.

Envy stepped out of the Hummer and faced his brother's truck with his hands raised in the air, with his long dreads hanging at his sides.

In his hand was nothing more than a blunt that was rolled so fat it looked like a mini roll of carpet. He took the sherm smoke and blew it to the air.

"Get yo ass out here nigga and don't do nothing stupid!"

***

Three hours later, Greed found himself in the basement of one of Envy's trap houses. His brother had had him cornered and at his mercy. Yet, he refused to show Envy any sign of apprehension. Instead, he chose to accept the invitation to have a sit down. Greed wanted to feel him out and see if he could detect snake in his blood like Mack was screaming, before he was killed.

"I don't give a fuck what you talkin' about or how many niggas you have wit you. We all was finna die, that's on my blood, nigga," Greed said, taking a sip of the Hennessy he had snatched out of his glove compartment, before getting out of his whip.

His brother had offered him some Champagne, but he

was a street nigga at heart. He didn't like drinking shit that didn't get him drunk and he didn't understand why other people did that. It was the same with smoking a cigarette. What was the use of smoking them if they didn't do nothing for you? He wondered.

Envy adjusted his shoulders and looked across the table at his little brother. He could fake the funk. They didn't get along.

Ever since Greed had stolen Jersey from under him when they were in high school, he had always felt some type of way about him. "What are you doin' back in New Jersey?"

In the back, the sounds of Tupac's *My Ambitions as a Rider* played through the speakers. The room they sat in was dark and illuminated by only a weak red-light bulb. It smelled rank. Like the men inside of it had not washed their asses in days. Greed never liked funky niggas. His. stomach was turning over and over again.

He took a sip from the bottle and swallowed the brown liquid that burned his belly. "Nigga, I am New Jersey. Ain't shit changed, and don't you forget it." He sat the glass down so hard that it nearly shattered.

Envy mugged him with his money green eyes. Curling his lip, he started to imagine his brother in a casket with a hundred shots in his face. He felt his sick coming on. First the itches, then body trembles. He tried so hard to fight his craving. The vision of sticking a syringe so far up his vein teased his mind. The temporary pain was nothing compared to the divine feeling he'd get once he fed the poison into his blood stream. Nothing in life gave him immense joy like heroin. He mugged Greed with hatred.

"Every fucking thing has changed, nigga. I run this muthafucka now! Don't shit come from here to New York without my stamp of approval. Now, why are you here?" He slammed his hand on the table so hard that it knocked over the bottle of Hennessy.

Luckily none spilled on Greed.

Greed scooted his chair back from the table and sipped the rest of his drink. He slowly looked up at his brother with hatred. Clenching his jaw off and on. His heart thumped in his chest as if it was trying to break out of it.

He looked around at all of the armed men and it got him even madder. "I see ain't too much changed. You still need a million and one niggas just to talk to little ole me. Ain't that a bitch?" He laughed and slammed his glass back on the table.

Envy lowered his head and mugged him with a death stare.

He didn't fear Greed. Never had, he simply feared breaking his promise to their father, Sin, that he would never kill him. It was his last dying wish.

Every time he saw Greed, it made it that much harder for him to hold up his end of things.

Envy took his .45 and slammed it on the table with the barrel pointed at Greed. He had visions of pulling the trigger. He could always chop his body into little pieces and throw them down the incinerator. No one would be the wiser. But he couldn't.

He hated that he believed in spirits. He knew that their father was in that room right then.

Greed curled his lip. "You got that muthafucka out, so what you gon' do with it?"

Both men mugged each other for a long time. No words were exchanged. Pac continued to spit in the background. The air was stale. Then the light bulb started to go out. Flickering off and on. Rats crawled across the floor. The pitter patter of their claws was the only noise outside of the music.

"I'm gon' give you one warning. I don't want you in my city. All that Cartel shit you did back in the day still got a bad taste in everybody mouth, including mine. Before you left Cali you already had a million-dollar bounty on your head. A bounty that's tempting for me to cash in. You know it's all about the money for me. I don't give a fuck about that bloodline shit. Blood don't pay the bills." His green eyes seemed to light up in the dark basement.

"I never did like to listen. That's why I got my ass whooped more than you did. It never worked, because I do what the fuck I wanna do and my blood is everything. That's what it's all about for me." He took the Glock out of the small of his back and slammed it on the table. The barrel pointed directly at Envy.

"We might as well do this shit right now, fuck playing all of these games. My people think it's over for me anyway, no harm no muthafucking foul."

The whole room seemed as if they cocked their weapons at once.

Envy held up his hand. "You sure that's what you wanna do?" He looked at his little brother closely. He was still impulsive. One day that would be his down fall, he was sure of it.

Greed placed his finger on the trigger of his weapon. "Fuck all this talking, nigga, let's get it." He was ready to meet The Reaper. There was no way he was going to allow his brother to pull a gun on him and he not do anything about it. Somebody had to die and it if it was going to be him, he was going to take his brother with him.

They heard a loud crash and then a big boom. Greed smiled.

All of the men started to scatter from the basement, but both brothers remained seated mugging each other.

Seconds later, they came back and slowly walked backwards with their hands in front of them. Greed didn't even turn around to see what they were looking at. He simply sat with a smile on his face, especially when he saw how big Envy's eyes got.

August kept his arm draped around Envy's baby mother's neck. He had taped four different bombs to her chest. In the dark basement, the digital clocks that ticked backwards lit up.

Aiden walked alongside of her with a shotgun to her head. "Yo, I think it's time y'all let my uncle up out this mafucka or we gon' be forced to blow this bitch up along wit everybody else, and that's including ourselves.

"You kill him, you gotta kill us, muthafucka," August said with his thumb over the detonator.

Envy's eyes got as big as paper plates. He wondered how they'd gotten a hold of his wife and how they located Greed. He looked over to his wife with a heavy heart. He started to get up, but sat back down from fear of them hurting her. He couldn't allow for that to happen. He felt trapped. He curled his lip and looked over to his brother with hatred.

Greed's smile widened. All of them had tracking devices on their phones and he was glad because of that. "That's what loyalty in my blood look like. You got a week to hand over my city and to leave this mafucka. Only a week. If you're still here by the end of that week, may the strongest man survive."

Envy watched as they led his wife out of the basement before unstrapping the bombs and pulling off in their vehicle, down the alley.

He swore to himself that he would get even and that before it was all said and done, he would kill his little brother.

His promise to their father would have to rest in peace.

***

Jersey hugged Stacey as she came into the kitchen to help her prepare the dinner table.

After she had gotten word that her husband was in danger, she'd sent her nephews to handle business. As soon as she gave them the order, she knew she didn't have anything to worry about.

She sent her prayers up to Jehovah and started to cook the biggest meal she could think of. It was the life they lived. No day was promised. It was all about making the best of the day they were in and she knew her position was most important.

While her husband handled that goon shit out in the field, she was the brains of things. Because even though he was very cunning, he was also extremely impulsive. So, where his impulses took over, her wisdom and strategies came in and finished the job thoroughly.

Every strong man needed an equally strong woman. It was ying and yang. A balance that God had put in place and nobody could conquer.

Stacey came into the kitchen and gave her a big hug, before kissing her on the cheek. "Momma, I need to talk to you and I don't want you to be mad at me." She whipped the mashed potatoes into a big white bowl and put saran wrap over it, taking it to the dining room table that was already covered in wrapped, steaming food. She was nervous and prayed that Jersey didn't tear into her ass for what she was about to tell her.

They were in a two story Victorian home that Jersey had inherited from her great grandmother. It had four bedrooms and three bathrooms. A decked-out basement and den, along with an attic. The kitchen was huge and fully furnished, everything modern.

Jersey looked at her from the side of her face. "What could you possibly have to tell me that would make you say all of that first?" She eyed the pretty girl closely.

"Can we go into the living room and sit for a moment before everybody gets here. I really need your guidance."

Her eyes lowered into slits. She looked at the clock on the wall and noted she had about an hour before everybody was set to show up for the obligatory Sunday dinner.

It didn't matter what was going on in their lives, the law was for every member of the family to be sitting at the dinner table by 7 on Sunday nights.

It was her job as the Queen of the bloodline to have everything prepared. She took it very serious, even if she was sick and unable to see straight, she would find a way to get into that kitchen to make it happen. It was not only her duty, but her joy.

"Let's go, Stacey, I can give you about fifteen minutes.

As soon as Jersey sat down, Stacey bounced up from the couch.

She paced in front of her, with her hands bent so that they rested on her lower back. Her long curly hair hung past her waist, all natural. She exhaled loudly.

Jersey frowned. "Lil' girl, I know you ain't call me in here just so you can huff and puff while you walk in front of me. You better say somethin' or I'm gon' go back to doin' what I was doin' in here for the family. Now spit it out." She was ready to stand up and wring the girl's neck. She hated when anybody disrupted her Sunday dinner preparations.

Stacey lowered her head in defeat. "Okay, mom, look, me and Ajani has been screwing around ever since I turned eighteen, well before then, but really screwing as of my 18th birthday. I really care..."

Jersey stood up and got into her face. "What the fuck you just say?"

Stacey felt like she was ready to shit on herself. She took a few steps backward. She didn't want any problems with Jersey. She had heard that Jersey was as much of a killer as the men in the family. She started to feel like telling her was a big mistake, but she felt it would be worse if the words left Averie's mouth first.

"Don't get to running. Repeat yourself." She lowered her eyes into slits. "Get over here and sit yo ass down." She pointed to the couch.

Stacey slowly came over and took a seat, scared out of her mind. "Okay, it's like I said. Me and him have been messing around heavy ever since my 18th birthday. And I..."

"Do Averie know about this? Does she know you fuckin' my son? Does she know that her little cousin, her own bloodline, is allowing the same dick that's running in and out of her, to fuck you, too? Do she?" Jersey could feel herself getting heated.

This sounded like betrayal to her. Disloyalty. Ratchet shit. Things she wasn't about to gee for, not as the head of the females of their family. She was definitely gon' make sure that Greed got on Ajani's ass.

"She knows because she gave us permission to do so."

Now Jersey's mind was completely blown. She couldn't understand what would make Averie give her that right. She just couldn't fathom her doing so. Jersey held up one finger.

"Sit yo ass down and I'll be back." She jogged up the stairs and went into the guest bedroom, waking Averie from her slumber.

Five minutes later, they were all in the living room, sitting on the couch.

"So yeah, Mom, I gave them permission to do it on her birthday because if I hadn't, they would have done it anyway. I just didn't know they were going to keep it up, or that she was going to get pregnant," she said this part so low that they barely heard her.

Jersey's eyes got so big that they looked like big snow balls with a little black dot on each one. "Bitch, you're pregnant?" She felt her heart thumping in her chest. She looked over the pretty girl and felt every type of anger known to man. She felt her whole body getting hot. She imagined what things looked like for her grandson and what his relation would be to the new baby and it was like her scalp blew off of her head like a choo choo train. She grabbed Stacey by the hair and flung her over the couch. Ripping her Ferragamo belt from around her own waist. "Hold this bitch still. I'm finna whoop her little pretty ass like I'm supposed to. Hold her, Averie, and you next!"

Averie grabbed Stacey's shoulders and pressed her firmer into the arm of the couch. She watched Jersey wrap the thick belt around her wrist before she raised it in the air.

Stacey felt the first lash whip across her naked ass after Jersey pulled her panties down, and she screamed. It felt like she had been sliced by a razor-sharp knife. The second blow landed in the same spot, causing her to try and run unsuccessfully because Averie was holding her down.

"You got the nerve to fuck my grandson's father?"

Whap!

"Then on top of that you get pregnant?

Whap!

"Didn't take into consideration what its gon' do to the family."

Whap!

"Then on top of that, we are forced to take yo ass in because you're carrying our bloodline within you?"

Whap!

"When I'm done with this ass, you gon' think everything through thoroughly."

Stacey felt the blows one after the next, crying so hard that the couch under her was drenched in tears. Her ass felt raw and she could feel the blood dripping down her thighs. Every blow felt like a cut by a razor blade and then Jersey went nuts, blow after blow.

Whap! Whap! Whap! Whap! Whap!

Again, and again. Over and over until her arm gave out. She grabbed a handful of Stacey's hair. "Now get your ass up them stairs and soak in the tub. I'll be up there in a minute to cleanse your wounds. You don't say nothing to the men of the family about this. Neither one of you. When y'all fuck up, we gon' handle this as women. You got me?" she said, looking from one girl to the next.

They both nodded with tears in their eyes. Averie was so terrified she didn't know what to do. She saw the rawness of her cousin's ass and wanted to jump out of a window. She didn't think she could handle that form of an ass whooping. In fact, she knew she couldn't.

Jersey pointed toward the steps. "Up, little girl. Right now!"

They watched Stacey slowly make her way up the stairs. Before she disappeared, she stopped. "Thank you, Momma." Stacy felt that Jersey could have come down a lot harder on her. She was thankful to still be alive. She nearly broke her neck to get out of the room and up the stairs.

Jersey turned to Averie. "What were you thinking?" She grabbed her hand and sat her on the couch.

Averie lowered her head. "Mom, I can't take that butt whooping that you just gave her. I'm not strong enough, honestly." She was dead serious.

Jersey shook her head. "Don't worry about that right now. You'll pay for your sins at another time. I need to know what's going on up here. Your cousin?"

Averie shook her head. "I really didn't have a say so. You know I love Ajani with all of my heart but I'm just not enough. He needs more, and they've been flirting and just doing the most way before I said it was okay. I felt that if I hadn't given the green light, it would have happened anyway and then I would have felt betrayed by the both of them."

Jersey raised her eyebrow. "And how do you feel now?" She shook her head.

"Absolutely the same."

Jersey grabbed her hand and kissed it. "Unfortunately, you've made that bed and now you have to lie in it with your son's father and your little cousin. You must stand firm, as a woman, handle your business to make sure that the family you started remains strong. Your bloodline starts with Jahni. He has to be your priority, but you must build a foundation around him that fits into all of this. If ever you become too weak to move forward, you have to let me know so we can figure things out together, because that baby growing inside of her makes her family and equal to you. I know you don't like to hear that but it's the truth."

Averie lowered her head. She felt defeated. Stacey lust-ing after Ajani was the nail in the coffin; stealing away all she felt she had in life.

The man she loved with all of her heart and the only family that had ever accepted her for who she was. Her heart felt like it was splitting in two.

"Just tell me you will always love me as your daughter, Momma, and that's enough for me, for now." She was on the verge of tears. She felt like her world was ending around her, like her security blanket being stripped away.

Jersey wrapped her into her warm embrace, and hugged her, before kissing her on the forehead. "You'll be my daughter. My loyalty for you is already sealed in blood. Ain't nothing gon' ever change that."

T.J. Edwards

Chapter 10

"Since I'm moving over to New York, I can give you this club right here as long as you got enough bread to keep it moving forward. I got twenty main bitchez here that get money. Now I can't promise you that they ain't gon' wanna follow me over there, but I will give you a chance to shoot yo shot at 'em. They already feeling yo lil' cute ass and that's gon' probably be your down fall," Vanity said, as she reached down and pulled Ajani's dick out of her. They had been up all night screwing. Ajani seemed as if he couldn't get enough of her treasures, tracking her down every single day since the day she'd given him the pussy four days ago.

She got out of the bed, slid into her robe and tied the sash around her waist.

Ajani stood up and stretched. His long dick swung from side to side, before he picked up his boxers and slid into them.

"That ain't gon' be my downfall. I know how to stand on my square. For me, it's all about the money. I'll never lose sight of that. I haven't this far."

Vanity went into her personal bathroom and started the shower. She could feel she was very sticky between her legs. His cum ran out of her and gave her a chill. She still couldn't believe they had did what they had. She felt a little guilty.

"I'm just telling you that once you enter into this sex industry that it's real hard for a person to stay grounded. You gotta look at these bitchez as paychecks. Fuck what they look like. Pussy gon' always be around until the end of time. Don't no bitch want a broke nigga. Bitchez will give you they life if they feel like you'll lead them in the right direction and make sure they're always straight. The worst man to follow is a muhfucka that don't know where he going. If ever a woman has to live paycheck to paycheck and she got a man, trust me every night before she goes to sleep, her thoughts are of resentment. She has no faith in him and when your woman loses faith in you as a man, you lose all control. And before it's all said and done, she will be plotting against you."

Ajani didn't know what she was talking about or where she was going with things. He didn't feel like he needed her prep talk. He already had his mind set on what he wanted to and what he wanted to do was make a lot of money while at the same time fucking a bunch of bad bitchez.

Money and sex. It was the only thing that made sense to him.

"TT, I got this shit. All you gotta do is show me the ropes a little bit." He snatched her up. "And keep putting this pussy on me. This the best I ever had." He stuck his hand between her legs and entered her with his fingers.

Vanity moaned and placed her hands on his shoulders while he dived in and out of her juice box. If all he wanted was one of her strip clubs, she would make it happen. After all, he was her favorite.

***

"Wake up, beautiful," Rayjon whispered, before kissing Averie on the forehead. He had quietly snuck into the guest bedroom after making sure everybody was still asleep. He had to see her.

She opened her eyes and when his face came into the view, the first thing she thought about was her morning breath. She refused to say anything. She could only imagine what held think, so she simply smiled.

Rayjon handed her a red rose and brushed her hair away from her face. To him she looked like the most beautiful woman in all the world.

He looked on the side of her and saw that Jahni was still asleep. He was glad that he hadn't awaken him. "Look, I just wanted to wish you a good morning and to give you that rose and this." He handed her a bundle of hundreds totaling ten G's. "I want you to go get a rental and find an apartment. Let them mafuckas know that you willing to pay up a whole years' worth of rent. Let me know what it's gon' cost and I got you. You hear me." He rubbed her forehead with his thumb. He felt that it was time for her to have her own place. He didn't expect for her and Jahni to stay living in a bedroom for too much longer. He wanted to put her on her feet the way she deserved to be.

"Damn! You so fine. I never knew that before."

Averie felt her heart flutter. She wanted to say thank you so bad, but her insecurity of her breath wouldn't allow it. Ajani had told her more than once that when she woke up in the morning to brush her teeth before she said anything to him. He told her that he hated a female's morning breath.

Rayjon heard a door open in the hallway, and shot to his feet.

"Look, just handle that business, if you want me to take you to the car rental place, I will. Just get you and him ready. I'll be back in an hour."

Five minutes later, he was closing the door to his bedroom, before loading his book bag with ten kilos of cocaine. He had to get shit back up and running like they had it before they left for California.

He had always had a heart for the streets, but his patience was short. He wanted large sums and he wanted them right away, which was why he preferred the Ski Mask way of living. But he also like to have his hustles spread out, which was why he was headed to where he was going.

Fifteen minutes later, he pulled into the alley of the duplex and four teenagers came out of the garage that he was parked in front of with pistols in their hands. The mugged his truck closely, as the snow began to fall.

Once Trigger saw him in the driver's seat, he threw his arms into the sky. "Yo, I know that ain't my big homie." He squinted his eyes and then looked more closely. Confirming it was Rayjon, he jumped into the air. "Hell yeah that's you. Nigga, what's happenin'?"

Rayjon got out of the truck and they embraced. He held the high yellow teen with the missing eye. Instead of Trigger rocking an eye patch over his left eye, he left it exposed.

He didn't give a fuck. He felt like he was never leaving New Jersey anyway and since every mafucka already knew him, he ain't have shit to hide.

He and Rayjon had gone to elementary school together.

Rayjon was two years older and had been present when Trigger killed his father for beating on his mother back in the day. When the law came fucking the hood up trying to capture his father's murderer, Rayjon had kept his mouth closed, and ever since then, he and Trigger had been tight.

The wind picked up and the snow started to really come down.

"Yo, what brings you over to these parts, kid?"

Rayjon watched him put his pistol back on his hip. As soon as he did, the other teens did the same thing.

"I told you that whenever I got right I was gon' reach for you. So that's why I'm here."

Trigger nodded his head. "Word is bond. Shit real clogged right now. We dealin' wit this drought that fucking up the flow that's coming out of New York. One of the bosses got pop wit twenty tons of that white, kid. Twenty! We ain't been able to cop shit since last Tuesday and the feinds mad crazy. They travelin' all the way to D.C. just to get right." He shook his head. "Yo, my bad." He turned to his lil' crew. "This my mans, Rayjon. Sun thorough through and through. I done seen the homie wit that steel and he get down. Mafuckas gotta respect kid because I love him. Point blank, that's my word, niggaz."

All three bandits nodded their heads at him. They looked like they could have been brothers. Short, stocky, with long ass dreads with different color J's on their feet.

Rayjon nodded back. "Loyalty, niggaz."

They threw up the L sign with their fingers. "Loyalty!" They seemed to say in unison.

Rayjon put his arm around Trigger's neck. "Like I was saying, I wanna put you where you need to be. I need to know what you can handle."

Trigger smiled and pulled the hairs on his chin. "I took over this whole hood, nigga. Chamber Courts is run by me, and I'll body any nigga that say different."

"Word is bond!" said one of the stocky niggaz.

Trigger adjusted his pistol. "I was on my way to copping a kilo. I was gon' buy it at eighteen and make fifty grand in about a week. I got a few traps around here jumping, but shit ain't really kick off until a week before the big drought. We had to move some niggaz around. Soon as they left, we opened up shop in their old traps but then my supply got jammed. The fiends are ready, it just we ain't got no product. I got thirty G's right now. Mafucka give me two for the thirty and I'm gone. Word is bond."

Rayjon turned the numbers over in his head. No matter what, he wouldn't be taking a loss because the kilos had come from a lick back in Cali. He wanted to make sure his lil' mans was out there eating and at the same time, he wanted to get his chips up, so he could low key make sure Averie and Jahni was straight. He wanted to see her in a nice place and rocking a fly ass whip. Not to mention, he felt that all women needed a certain amount of pocket change. She deserved it in his eyes, and he was gon' make sure she had it. Not only that, but he had a few other business interests in mind.

"Yo, give me that thirty and I'm gon' give you four kilos of some fire. You pricing them at fifty apiece. That's two hundred G's that you gon' make off of thirty. Not only that but after you do your thing, I'ma pop you bricks at fifteen apiece. All thirty-six, all powder. You put your own steps on 'em."

Trigger took a step back and looked him over closely. The snow was falling so hard that they could barely see in front of them. The wind picked up and Trigger felt his nose freezing over. He pulled Rayjon into a half a hug. "I'll body a whole family for you, my nigga. Word is bond ever since I met you, you been one hunnit. "

***

"Where you finna go?" Ajani asked Averie as she slipped fresh Timbs on to their son's feet and cuffed his Gucci pants so that they fit over the top of them. He noted that she had their child looking fresh.

"I'm going out apartment hunting. I want us to get our own place so that your moms and pops can have their own space. I feel like we're somewhat of a burden to them, you know with our situation and all."

She brushed past him carrying Jahni's coat. As soon as she got close enough she could smell the scent of fucked pussy all over him and it made her want to throw up. She knew for a fact he had not been home all night, so it couldn't have been Stacey's cat.

She simply shook her head.

Apart of her wanted to snap out, but an even bigger part just didn't care anymore. She wanted to see Rayjon so bad that it was killing her. At least with him, there would some form of respect and kindness.

Ajani scrunched his face. "You crazy as hell. It just started snowing. I ain't finna go out there and drive you around nowhere and you ain't taking my whip. You better ask my brother when he get back to see if he will. Plus, I'm tired as a muthafucka." He plopped on the bed and as soon as he did, the scent of his unwashed body floated into the air.

Averie gagged. She felt ready to puke. "Seriously, Ajani, you gotta go in there and wash yo ass. You smell horrible. I don't know what bitch you been fucking all night, but you stank."

He shrugged his shoulders. "I will when I get up. I'm worn out right now. I can't even think straight. That's why I can't take you nowhere, but I know bro will. He always telling me how much I should appreciate you and all that shit, so he can step in and make sure you feel like it. It ain't enough hours in a day. I'm tired. I need to…" He started to snore right away.

Averie simply shook her head before opening a window.

She could not understand how he could treat her that way.

She had given him his first child and held him down

through some of the roughest of times and in exchange, all she'd asked of him was for him to love her and come home at night. She didn't think that asking too much, but the way he had destroyed her self-esteem, she felt she wasn't even worth it.

Rayjon had arrived two hours later and picked her up. They rolled around the city for three hours straight looking over possible places of residence. She was trying to make sure she picked a safe area. Her main concern was the welfare of her son. New Jersey was crime ridden. Drugs had taken over and majority of city was an unsafe place to reside.

Finally, the last stop out on Woodside seemed appropriate. The realtor was a very nice Arab lady, who seemed to be very respectful.

The property was a two story, red bricked home, with three bed rooms and two baths. A big backyard and a two-car garage.

She wanted seventeen hundred a month, and that didn't include utilities. Averie's eyes bugged out of her head. She felt it was way out of her price range, until Rayjon patted her on the back and told her to go and wait in the car with Jahni.

Soon as she was out of sight, he pulled the Arab woman aside.

"I want to pay up a full year's rent right now and I don't want you to allow her to place anyone else on the lease other than her and the child. If you will accept those terms, I can assure you that your property will be taken care of. And when it is time for the lease to be renewed, we will do another year upfront. How does that sound?"

Even though she barely spoke English, money translated the same in every culture.

Five minutes later, Averie was signing the lease and given the keys to the property.

They sat down at Coachella's, a five-star restaurant located in the heart of the city. There was light jazz playing when they entered into the place. The lights were already low and one of the Maître'd's approached them with a white cloth draped across his forearm. He handed menus that did not include the prices of their meals.

Rayjon pulled out her chair before she sat in it. It took her a little while to grasp what he was trying to do. She had never had a man pull out her chair before. She felt flattered and like she wasn't worth all of that.

"Gone head and sit down, ma." He waited until she bent her knees and then pushed the chair under her.

Averie blushed and almost couldn't look across the table at him. She just couldn't understand why he treated her so nice. She felt like she didn't have anything to offer him. Like she was damaged goods. In her own opinion, her body was shot, her vagina couldn't have been the tightest and she had more baggage than the Greyhound bus station. She wondered if he was just taking pity on her.

Rayjon looked across the table and saw flashes of his mother. A strong black female that had the weight of the world on their shoulders.

He had known Averie since she was fifteen years old. He'd watched her blossom into a woman and that's with all of the things that she had been through with their family.

She lowered her head. "What do you really want from me, Rayjon? Keep in mind that I don't have anything other than a whole lot of baggage. So, what gives?"

Rayjon shrugged his shoulders. "Averie, I already know that it's crazy that I'm here with you right now, but why not? I mean in all honesty who are we hurting and who the hell cares?"

They took a moment to order their food. Rayjon requested a bottle of Merlot, knowing that Averie often sipped on it with his mother. That was their little drinky-drink, as they called it.

"I don't know. I guess I just feel uncomfortable because I don't feel like I deserve any of this. I ain't nothing but a baby momma. I'm supposed to expect the bare minimum, and this is definitely way more than that."

"Why do you have to think like that, though? Why can't you just accept the fact that you are royalty? That you are a strong, beautiful black queen. Why can't you let me make sure that you're straight, because it ain't hard for me to do that. Especially since I know that you're worth it. You ain't never crossed me. You ain't never crossed nobody in my family. You told my brother where you were going tonight, right?"

She nodded. "Yeah, because you told me to."

"Okay, and what did he say?" Rayjon asked as the bottle of wine was sat on the table. He pulled out the cork and sucked the juices off of it.

"He said he wanted to handle some business with Stacey anyway. That he didn't feel like me being all under him because he wanted to enjoy her fresh, pregnant pussy." Averie thought back on how that made her feel and she just couldn't stop herself from breaking down. "I don't know why he treats me the way that he does. I've never done anything, but try my best to be there for him against all odds. How can he hate me so much and then go so hard to get me back from Game? I mean, what was that all about? Why not just let him kill me?"

When Rayjon imagined her being killed, it made him feel like bodying something. He would never allow for that to happen for as long as he lived. He didn't want to tell her that he was the one that put the plan into action to get her back from her captors.

"To be honest with you, Rayjon, I just want to be happy. That place that you got me today is the first step. I think once I get into my own space and I'm able to get my mind together that I will become stronger. Right now, I am simply mentally exhausted." She rubbed her temples and blinked tears. She felt like she was on the verge of a mental break down.

Rayjon came around the table, knelt down and took her hand. "Look, just let me be your best friend through all of this and we'll figure the rest out together. I got you. But I need for you to have yourself as well because I can't do all of this on my own. I need you just as much as you need me trust me." He lifted her chin and rubbed her bottom lip with his thumb. "I think you look beautiful tonight, too. Rocking Prada like you rocking it. They should be paying you to promote they shit." He smiled, and she couldn't help but to do the same.

T.J. Edwards

Chapter 11

"Please! Please! Please! I am begging you! Stop it! Stop it! You're killing him!" Pam hollered with mascara running down her face. She was about to lose her mind as she watched the muscle-bound man slice her husband to shreds.

Paul felt the blade go into his stomach and rip upward. It felt like everything within him was falling out of his center. It wasn't even painful, it was more exhausting than anything else. Before he could fully process what was being done to him his soul escaped his body and left him lifeless.

Greed turned around to face the Federal Judge.

He had blood all over his black apron. "I don't know what you did to Kabir Alameen, but you better make it right or your kids are next." He snatched the little boy up by the throat and slung him down on top of the table. "My client tells me that you have something against him and since you do, I have something against you. So, what we're going to do is make a big splash so that the rest of the higher ups know to take my client very serious."

She got up to run to the table, but Aiden slammed her back into her seat aggressively. "Please don't kill my grandson." She whimpered. "He doesn't have anything to do with anything to do with any of this. He's just a six-year-old child. I am begging you."

Greed raised the meat cleaver. "Yeah hold that thought. And take a good look at this hit." He brought the cleaver down at full speed until the blade landed on the little boy's chest, busting it wide open.

He could hear him screaming through the duct tape. He raised it again, and brought it down even harder.

He had already blocked it out of his mind that he was

killing a kid and simply saw the little brat as a job that had to be completed. Very seldom was he able to stop and think about who it was that he was killing. There was to be no emotions in his line of work.

He learned that a long time ago that emotions would get you killed or locked up later on.

Greed open and dug into his body ripping out his heart. Kabir had given him the order that he needed to see the child's heart in his hands before he could say that the mission was a success. He didn't know why he needed all of that but he gave him what he wanted.

He positioned the laptop and held the little boy's heart up in front of the camera, squeezing it so that blood squirted into the air.

Pam fainted and Aiden smacked fire from her face. She fell to the floor and he pulled her up by her hair and slung her back into the chair. Wrapping his fingers into her hair until his knuckles were resting against her scalp.

Greed took the little boy and pushed his lifeless body onto the floor. He looked over at Pam, after adjusting the laptop. Kabir's face appeared on the screen.

"They say the eyes of Lady Justice are supposed to be blind. Maybe if you were, you wouldn't have prejudged me and forced my innocent family to be shipped back to our warring country. You support to destroy D.A.C.A., and not only that, you're shooting for me to be slain in this system when I am an innocent man. I have done no wrong to you or your country. So why do you persecute me?"

Aiden yanked on her hair so hard that he ripped out a hand full of bloody roots. "Answer him!"

Pam was out of breath. She was starting to become hysterical. She looked down and saw her grandson's body and nearly lost her mind. He was dead, and it was all her fault.

Then she looked over at her husband.

She looked into the screen with tears in her eyes. "They told me you were on the watch list and that you were a well-known suspected terrorist. There are pictures of you colluding with major official of ISIS. Money was traced, things were confirmed. My hands were tied."

Kabir frowned into the camera and shook his head. "My business is not to be discussed. I said the eyes of Lady Justice are supposed to be blind, so that is how I want you." He nodded at Greed.

Aiden held her head back as Greed waltzed over with the ice pick in his hand. He held the point right over her left eye, looking down on her with a slight smile on his face. He hated judges in all shades and hues and genders.

He felt no sympathy for the woman. He felt he was about to give her what she deserved and nothing less than that. He cocked his arm back and got his aim together.

"Ahhhhhh! Whhyyy!" Pam felt the point of the object stab into her eye and the pain that ensued made her want to die immediately.

It was unbearable. She felt the man digging into her socket and then her ball was being extracted from her face. It felt like he was pulling out her brain through the small socket. All she could do was scream at the top of her lungs while the man that was holding her laughed at the top of his lungs. She felt blood running down her cheek.

Greed wrapped the umbilical cord looking tendon around his wrist and pulled, yanking Pam's eye all the way from the socket. Blood oozed out of the hole in her face.

"Please! I am begging you. I will make you a very rich man. Millions. Whatever it takes. Just please don't kill me, I don't deserve it. You shouldn't hold me responsible. I will do anything." She whimpered out of breath.

She could feel the cord that once held her eye lying across her cheek like a hot piece of spaghetti. One entire side of her face throbbed. Reminding her of the excruciating torment.

On the laptop, Kabir smiled. "Everybody begs for mercy when the heat is on. How many people have you shown mercy to? Do you care about them falsely accusing me? All of you were ready to throw away my life and for no reason!" he boomed into the screen. His entire body was shaking uncontrollably.

Pam was out of breath and in so much pain that she begged silently for death. The man behind her had a handful of her hair and every time she moved in the least bit.

"Please, spare me. Anything you want, and I'll make it happen. Give me that chance," she mostly whispered because she was out of breath. She felt woozy and her living room was staring to fade out.

Greed smacked her hard, jolting her awake. He took the ice pick and jammed it into her other eye, poking it so hard that it squirted blood. He smashed the pick into her face with all of his might and started to dig the eye out.

"Arrrrgh! Arrrrgh! I can't. Take. It!" Pam screamed as she felt her eye explode.

Her body shook uncontrollably, and she could feel the blood pouring down her neck. She could hear the sound of a man's laughter.

Greed dug her eye out of her face and showed it to Kabir on the screen. He rolled the two balls around the palm of his left gloved hand.

"Mission accomplished. Dead or alive?" he asked, looking over his shoulder at her.

Kabir sat back on his prison bed and frowned, having control of a person's life was the ultimate power in his book. An American judge. White. In her million-dollar home, right after dinner. It was what most Arabs dreamt about. To kill a white American of power period and though he couldn't do it with his own two hands, he was going to sit back and enjoy every second of it.

"Dead and in the most vicious way," he hissed.

Greed nodded at Aiden. Aiden smiled, placed his big hands on each side of Pam's head and quick as a rabbit started to twist it with all his might. He held the back of her head and chin and twisted it around and around on her shoulders. The sounds of her bones popping was so loud in the room that it sounded like a bunch of campers stepping on twigs in the woods.

Pam heard the order for her death and pissed on herself.

Death. Death. Oh my, God. They are going to kill me, she thought.

Finally, she felt the man's hands grab her head roughly, then he started to twist. When it got to the point where it wasn't supposed to turn anymore, he forced it and she heard the loudest pop in the world. It was followed by the worst pain she had ever imagined.

Greed stabbed her all over the face again and again. Honestly, he was bored with the entire murder. He had Envy on his mind. He knew deep down in his heart that he was going to have to kill him. A part of him had always known that his brother had been jealous of he and Jersey's relationship since day one.

After getting word that he'd been talking to the Feds, Greed knew right away that he was going to kill him.

Snitches got ditches, he thought to himself and smiled.

Pam's face looked like a bashed in jack o' lantern. Her mouth was wide open, and her head hung oddly at her side.

The room smelled of blood and death. Scents that had Aiden with a hard on.

***

Boom!

Trigger kicked the door in so hard that it slammed against the wall and the knob left a hole in it. He ran into the house with Rayjon behind him holding two .44 Desert Eagles.

There were three dudes and two females sitting on the couch in the living room playing a video game. After the door had been kicked in they jumped into the air and got ready to run out of the room.

"Everybody, lay the fuck down now or I'ma start chopping shit."

They dropped to the floor and covered their heads. The females were already crying and whimpering. Nobody wanted to die and all of them feared for their lives.

Rayjon adjusted his mask and pointed the guns at the victims. He didn't want to be in there too long. He wanted Trigger to make a statement and for them to be right back out. He had a bad feeling about this particular move.

"Everybody, turn the fuck over and look up at me. Now!" Trigger ordered, cocking the big shotgun. He had five shots and dead set on using every bullet if he had to. He felt that all people understood was bloodshed. He watched them flip on to their backs, whimpering like babies in a daycare. It made him sick.

Rayjon eyed the scene closely, watching Trigger's every move, ready to step in and speed shit along if he had to. In his mind, there was no point to the move because they weren't pulling a kick doe to get money but to send a message. This had been the ninth one in the same day. He understood triggers strategy, but he didn't agree with it. Trigger insisted that he had to be present so that he could see how he got down when in all actuality Rayjon really didn't give a fuck how he got down just as long as the numbers were right.

"Yo from now on ain't nobody selling shit at this trap unless they pushing my shit. This is my hood and every penny coming through this mafucka belong to me. Do everybody in this room get that?" Trigger said, pointing the barrel of the shotgun from one person to the next.

"Yeah!" they agreed in unison.

He could see them shaking as if there wasn't any heat on in the house. All their eyes were bucked. That made him smile under his mask.

"If I hear about anything getting moved in this hood without it crossing me first, I'm bodying whole families. Bitches and kids included. You hoes hear me?" He put the shotgun to their heads one by one.

They closed their eyes as if they were waiting for the blasts to come out of the gun to knock their heads off.

One female was shaking so bad it looked like she was having a seizure. Her whole body vibrated, then her eyes rolled into the back of her head and she started to choke.

This freaked Trigger out. "Yo, what the fuck wrong wit this bitch?" He jumped back and mugged the shit out of her.

"Oh my, God!" said one high yellow girl with freckles all over her face. She looked like she was about to panic. "She's having a fucking seizure again. Somebody gotta get me a spoon, so I can hold her tongue or she gon' choke to death." She looked up at Trigger.

He frowned. "Man, fuck that bitch! Far as I'm concerned she can die. That ain't got shit to do wit' me."

The yellow girl started crying right away. "She's my sister. Please don't do this. Please just let me..."

"Bitch, I don't give a fuck! Lay yo punk ass down or word is bond, I'm about to blow yo shit up all the way back," he growled through clenched teeth.

He was seconds away from knocking her brains out of her scalp. He could care less about the sick girl. To him, death was a natural part of life. He didn't feel like it was his job to be savior of the world.

Rayjon did all he could not to pay attention to the way the girl was flopping around on the floor, but he simply couldn't ignore it.

He dropped to his knees and stuck his hand into her mouth, taking a hold of her tongue to make sure she didn't choke on it. He was all for making a statement, but he wasn't cool with allowing a young girl to die just because she was sick. It wasn't her fault and it wasn't their intention to kill anybody unless they had to. He couldn't see himself allowing her to die and that was that.

Ellie flopped around on the carpet while he held his hand on her chest to calm her. Thankfully, he was clearing her airwaves and holding her tongue because she had a habit of choking every time she had a seizure.

Slowly but surely the attack passed, and she calmed down until she was laying on the floor with beads of sweat peppered across her forehead. Her beautiful face frowned and casually straightened out.

Her sister, Bird, had tears in her eyes. "Thank you, kid. Word is bond, you just saved my sister's life. That's one hunnit, blood, fa' real" She hugged his leg.

Trigger mugged the entire scene. "Yo, what the fuck just happened, sun?"

He didn't know what to say or do. On the one hand, he wanted to continue to put his foot down, but then on the other, he was confused because he didn't know how to check Rayjon or if he was supposed to.

He thought about his daughter who had epilepsy the first four years of her life until she eventually grew out of it. There were times when she nearly choked to death, had his baby mother not been around to save her.

He imagined her having a seizure and his big homie saving her life. His heart grew warm and he finally understood. Rayjon to him was a true G. It took a real nigga to get down like he just had. He watched him step behind him after rubbing the little girl's cheek.

"A'ight, but like I said, this trap gon' only push my product." He took his mask off. "If any mafucka got anything to say about it, you tell them Trigger bringing that action. Word is bond—to the death, too. I'll be back to get y'all situated. Any questions?"

The entire room remained silent.

Chapter 12

"Gon', boy. Ugh get yo ass off of me. I ain't even on that shit right now." Averie said, pushing at Ajani's chest, just as he straddled her body with his shirt off.

He squeezed her titties inside the silk gown, then pushed them together, running his thumbs across the globes trying to locate her nipples.

"Shut yo ass up. If I wanna play wit these mufuckas, then that's what I'm gon' do and quit fronting like you don't want me to." He yanked her straps down fully exposing her then locating and pulling on her nipples.

Averie smacked his hand away. "Get the fuck off me and stop playing before you wake up Jahni. He just got to sleep, and I don't feel like being up with him all night." She tried to get up, but he pushed her back down to the bed.

Mugging her with obvious irritation. "Yo, so that's what you finna be on?" He felt himself becoming hot. He didn't like her refusing him, it was a shot at his ego

Averie sat up and politely pushed him off of her. Placing her straps back on to her shoulders, after stuffing her breasts back inside because she had no sexual desire for him at all.

Ajani had her emotions all out of whack. The last thing on her mind was sex, especially with him. She fluffed her pillows by punching it a few times, then turned on her side and tried to get comfortable with her back to him.

Ajani got to his knees and looked her over closely. He was stunned. "Oh, bitch, you got to be tripping. You think you finna be laid up in here and you ain't doing shit. You ain't giving up no pussy or nothing? Yo, you gotta get up out of here then on some real shit. Stacey finna take that spot. Get up!"

He grabbed her by the gown before pushing her out of the bed. His irritation had gotten the better of him. He wanted her to get the fuck away from him.

Averie landed on the floor and hit her elbow's funny bone. Her entire right arm felt like it was frozen. It hurt like hell. Before she could gather herself, Ajani turned the lights on in the guest bedroom, opened the closet and threw clothes at her.

Tears started to pool down her cheeks almost immediately. She got to her knees and watched him. "What are you doing, Ajani?"

"Bitch, you gettin' the fuck outta here. You had me tearing Los Angeles up for yo ass and this the thanks I get? You wanna act all funny with that popped ass body. Acting like you some type of model or something. News flash, shorty, yo stock done hit rock bottom. Only reason you sleepin' in this mufucka is because of my son. If it was up to me, I'd have your cousin in this bitch, folded up taking this dick. And I'd never try and hit that old ass pussy. Got the nerve to turn me down. Yeah, you up out this mufucka." He threw a shirt at her and it smacked her in the face.

Not only did it smack her in the face, but it hit her in the left eye and it stung like crazy.

Averie lowered her face to the floor and cried her eyes out. His words cut her like a knife. It hurt so bad that she wanted to die.

In that moment, she made up her mind that she was going to take her own life. She no longer wanted to live, even the thought of her son wasn't enough to make her want to go on. The pain was simply too much. She figured when he grew up he would adopt the same opinion of her that his dad had.

Ajani threw all her clothes out of the closet. They surrounded her as if they were a pile of leaves.

"What the fuck you sitting there crying for? Get yo monkey ass up and get the fuck outta of my parents' crib. You dismissed, bitch, I don't even give a fuck if you take your happy ass back to California. To be honest, you just dead weight. I should've let hat nigga body yo selfish ass." He curled his lip.

His last comment hurt him a little bit. He felt deep down that saying that way too harsh, but his ego wouldn't allow him to apologize.

Averie lowered her head then slowly stood up, her face wet with tears. Now her heart was completely broken. Split. Ripped in two by a man that she loved with all her heart and soul. She had honestly given him all that she was as a woman and the fact that he treated the way he was completely mind-boggling to her.

She felt lower than dirt, like trash that had been burned or snot in somebody's tissue. As a woman she felt stripped of her femininity. Like a nothing and nobody all at once. She couldn't even look in his face.

"Been trying to provide for yo ass ever since we started fucking around in high school. You ain't never gave me shit but a muthafucking headache. All this whiney shit all the time. You ain't never happy or satisfied and every little thing throw yo whole entire mood off and I'm just sick of it. I don't give a fuck what you do, but I want you out of here and away from my bloodline." He meant every word.

Averie dropped back to her knees and held her hands out at her sides, with her face bowed to the ground. Suddenly her reality kicked in. Her motherly instinct told her that she needed to fight harder, if not for her, then for her son. If Ajani broke all ties with her, where would that leave their child, she wondered.

She placed her forehead to the floor in total submission. Every part of her wanted to fight against the process and tell him to go fuck himself. To remind him that it was her body that brought their son into the world and that she almost died delivering him. That if nothing more she deserved his honor and respect for that.

But her only words to him were, "I'm sorry, baby. I am so, so sorry. Please forgive me because I need you. I can't make it in this world without you and our son needs you. Why would we hurt him like that when he is so innocent and pure?"

Ajani mugged her like she had lost her mind. This was a completely different person than the one from a few moments ago. Just seeing her bowed down to him like that irritated him even more. Now with the light on, he could see the stretch marks that decorated her titties. He remembered back when she didn't have any, and that small imperfection made him imagine what her entire body looked like.

The stretch mark across her stomach, the few that decorated her thighs and how flabby her breasts looked after she finished breast feeding their son. They were so flabby now and no longer perky the way he liked. He felt disgusted and didn't give a fuck how she felt or where she went.

"You can take Jahni wit you until we work something out, but I ain't even in no rush 'cause I got plenty of building to do. Far as you and I go, we through. I'll never get between them thighs again. I ain't trying to fuck wit Stacey on that level either, 'cause y'all got the same blood and I see what y'all turn into after the kids." He made a disgusted face. "So, get yo shit and get the fuck out."

Averie felt the snot pool out of her nostrils, she could barely breathe. The worst pain in the world had not been childbirth. It turned out to be the pain and utter disrespect from a man that she had given her all to. She felt like breaking down to her knees and balling her eyes out.

***

"Nigga, I'm on something. You can help her move all that shit over there. I done did my part," Ajani said, starting his Bentley. "On some real shit, big bro, you got the type of heart to care for bitchez like that and I don't. I wanna care, but I can't. I need you to care for me, because I just can't do it."

He looked out the window and saw Averie loading the last box in the big U-Haul truck. He felt a twinge of guilt. She really was a good girl, he just liked fresh pussy and new bodies. Strippers and all things exotic, her pussy was old news and he couldn't get past that.

Rayjon handed him the blunt after taking four strong pulls and inhaling strongly. He knew he wasn't about to chill with his brother too long because he had a whole lot of work to do in helping her move. He looked out the window at her and smiled.

The snow flurried around them. Wind blowing the few red leaves on the surrounding trees until eventually they came off and floated through the air. There was a long silence in between them, both men watching Averie close the back of the U-Haul before going back in, probably to get the Jahni.

"I care about her, bro," Rayjon said, watching her walk up the steps and disappear.

Ajani took a strong pull from the blunt and inhaled, holding the smoke before blowing it back out.

"You know I figured that. I see how you look at her like she a queen or something. That's the same way I used to see her before my brain got fucked up, up here." He touched his forehead with his pointy finger and curled his lip.

"N'all, kid, I'm saying I wanna fuck wit her on that level, if not right now, then somewhere down the line. I got some shit in me that addicted to Averie. I wanna hold her down and stand tall on my gangsta for her."

Ajani frowned and looked at him closely. "Really?"

He felt like his brother had to be bugging because from as far back as he could remember Rayjon always kept a bad bitch that was damn near flawless. He couldn't for the life of him imagine what he saw in Averie. She lost her appeal to him after the milk left her breast. He had no more physical attractions to her whatsoever. He even tried to fall in love with her maternal body, but no matter what he did it just didn't work.

"Yeah, I need your blessings, so that I can fuck wit her on that level. And it's deeper than sex, kid." Rayjon felt that as much as he desired Averie, he would never cross his brother like that. If Ajani wasn't cool with them fucking around, then he would let the matter go right away, because at the end of the day his little brother was his heart.

Ajani replayed all the good times he had with Averie in his mind's eye. He thought back to their high school days and any memories that would make him feel some type of way for her, but nothing worked.

At the end of the day for him it was all about new pussy and hers was not. He still cared about her and figured that if she had to be with somebody else it was good that it would be his brother. At least he wouldn't have to worry about a bunch of bitch niggas being around his son.

"You know what, big bro, if you feel like you can love her and take care of her, then you got my blessing. She deserves a nigga like you. I wish I could be him, but I' not. I ain't got them type of feelings in me no more and that's fucked up. I should've never looked down at her pussy while Jahni was coming out. That ruined shit for me." He shook his head in defeat.

Rayjon nodded. "Word is bond, I'ma hold her down the way I'm supposed to. I see a lot of our mother in her and that's gon' keep me honest. Besides all that, she really is a good woman. I just gotta build her up a lot, because she don't believe in herself and that's a problem."

Ajani shook his head. "Word is bond. Life is too short, kid. I'm trying to fuck and have bitchez, keep it moving. I ain't got time for all that sentimental shit. I feel like a nigga can't get rich if he got a bitch latched onto him."

He took another pull from the blunt and passed it to Rayjon. "Shorty yo problem now, bro. I wash my hands of her all across the board. Gotta find me some new pussy after I have Stacey get rid of that kid she carrying."

Chapter 13

"Well, that seem like it's everything. Thank God that's over," Averie said, looking around her new place.

She and Rayjon had just finished moving everything in and getting it situated to her liking. She noted that she had to get more furniture to give her home that *cozy* feel, but other than that it felt good to her to have her own place. She walked over and turned the heat up on the thermostat, trying to get rid of the winter chill.

Rayjon walked up behind her and wrapped her in his embrace, before kissing her on the forehead. "How do you feel and keep it one hunnit wit me, too."

Her perfume wafted up his nose intoxicating him. It was mixed with her natural scent and that drove him crazy.

She shrugged her shoulders. "I don't really know yet. I mean I am a little scared because this is basically the first time I have ever been on my own. So, it's spooky. I just don't wanna fail. Jahni needs me."

She was thankful the rent was paid for the entire year, so that would be the least of her worries. She also had about eight thousand dollars left over from the knot Rayjon had given her.

Ajani had offered to give her a few thousand and she turned him down.

Rayjon looked down into her beautiful face and smiled. He couldn't understand why she had him feeling some type of way, but he had to admit she really did. He guessed it was the fact she was so vulnerable and didn't have anybody to really protect her. The fact that she needed him and gave him purpose.

He also could not deny how bad she was to him. He loved everything about her face and body. He found her incredibly sexy. A woman he didn't feel he would ever get sick of. *How could he?* he wondered.

"Why you starin' at me like that?" she asked, starting to panic.

She wondered if he regretted standing by her side. He told her that he and Ajani talked about their situation and Ajani gave him the green light if he chose to take it.

She didn't even know what that looked like and even though she loved him for standing by her, she didn't think a relationship was in their best interest. She figured the family would never accept it.

"I ain't gotta have a specific reason to be admiring yo lil' fine ass. Right now, I'm just digging you and trying to appreciate your beauty. You ain't always gotta be on defense. You can let go when it comes to me." He kissed her on the forehead again, then leaned down and sucked on her neck, biting her particular spot before sucking forcefully.

Averie felt chills go down her spine, then the hair on the back of her neck stood up. She felt Rayjon cup her big booty and pull her more firmly into him. His breath smelled of spearmint, his cologne was Burberry Fresh, and he smelled clean. She didn't know why she focused on that aspect, but it turned her on.

She felt him squeeze her ass, then he slid his hand underneath and rubbed her kitty through the tight Prada pants.

"Umm, baby, you trying to get something started?" She popped back on her legs.

Rayjon guided her back to the wall and made her put her palms against it as if she was getting searched. He pulled her pants down along with her panties. He watched as she kicked both to the side. Her ass jiggled during the movements which turned him on.

He dropped to his knees and moved her legs apart. Her ass cheeks slightly brushed against his forehead. Rayjon could smell her pussy really well now. It was like an invitation to celebrate her body. Her scent appealed to the hungry male in him. He smashed his face into her crease and inhaled deeply, before separating her wet sex lips and sliding his tongue in between. She tasted salty at first, then like nothing at all. Her juices ran down his chin and traveled to his neck.

Averie poked her ass all the way out and moaned. She loved when Rayjon played with her down there because he always seemed to know what to do. She felt his tongue enter her hole and it made her spread her ass cheeks apart for him.

"Umm. Please heal my mind, Rayjon." She could already feel the tears pooling down her cheeks.

Rayjon took his tongue and ran it from Averie's clit, all the way up and in between her ass crack, before he trapped her clit with his lips and sucked the juices directly from her jewel. He could feel her shaking. She moaned so loud that he wanted to stroke his dick.

"Rayjon, Rayjon. If. You. Keep. Doing. That. I'm about to cum. I'm about to cum so fucking haarrd!" She felt him slide two fingers into her, running them in and out at full speed. Hard, not soft like he was afraid to thug-finger fuck that pussy. His brutality made her shake and scream at the top of her lungs.

Rayjon felt her squirting into his mouth and he swallowed it all. He picked her up and aided her down in front of the fireplace, after getting it going. She seemed to watch his every move until he was straddling her and taking off his shirt revealing a rock-hard body, full of tats.

Averie looked up at him as he unsnapped her bra in the front, exposing her breasts.

Rayjon took her bra and threw it to the side. He was fascinated by how her pretty brown nipples stood up thick and heavily engorged. Her tits were a caramel brown, nice and round. He didn't hesitate to squeeze them together before sucking all over them. The noises he made while doing his thing was enough to drive her insane.

"Huh—umm. Shit!" she moaned.

She felt him laying her back, kissing down her chest. Before he got to her stomach, she tried to push him away from her. She didn't want him to feel the stretchmarks and get turned off. She didn't know what she would do if she found a way to disgust him. Ajani had screwed her mind all the way up.

Rayjon gave her a look of confusion. "What's the matter?"

His dick was so hard it throbbed against his stomach. He wanted to be ten inches deep in her pussy. He felt like he couldn't remember what it felt like.

Averie felt ready to panic. "Just umm. Well, umm. You know after I had Jahni my stomach, ain't. Well, I should have used more cocoa butter, but I just don't want you to feel like you gotta..."

Rayjon pushed her backwards, lowered his head and kissed what he deemed as her perfect stomach. He took his tongue and traced each individual stretchmark and kissed them.

"This body is beautiful. This is a perfect temple, one worth cherishing and indefinitely appreciating. You are a goddess, you brought a child into this world, something no man can ever do. I'm going to worship this perfect temple and show you how a real nigga supposed to hold you down." He nipped at her stomach with his teeth before sucking and kissing all over it.

Trailing his tongue downward until he came to her sex lips, they were freshly trimmed. Her lips puckered, so he trapped one sex lip in his mouth and sucked while his thumb ran across her erect clitoris. She pumped her hips from the floor and moaned with her head tilted backward. His fingers invaded her pussy causing her to open her legs more.

"Rayjon. Please. Just get up here and make love to me. No fucking, no trying to hurt me, just help me to heal. I need you deep inside of me. Please." Tears fell down her cheeks, emotionally. She was a wreck and needed to become one with him on a new liberated level.

The more he touched her the weaker she became. She wanted to give him her body. For the first time, she had a man inside of her that actually cared about her and saw her as beautiful after having Jahni.

So, every time Rayjon sucked or licked a certain portion of her body, it felt amplified.

Rayjon slid up her body and put his fat dick head at her hot opening. Her kitty seemed to be trying to suck him inside. He rubbed the head up and down her slit until she moaned loudly, spreading her thick thighs wide.

He watched them jiggle some and it made his dick throb. "You want me, Averie?"

She reached between her legs and pinched her clit, then squeezing her pussy lips together before opening them all the way. She slid her middle finger into herself and moved it in and out in anticipation for him. She yearned for his meat so bad.

"Please, Rayjon, I need you! Please give me that dick. I need it so bad." she whimpered, as she slid two fingers deep within herself and humped them.

Rayjon stroked his dick as he watched her. He couldn't control the crazy urges going through him. He slid his fingers into her and then sucked them into his mouth, tasting her. "You sure you want me?" He put his fat head on her sex lips after pulling her fingers out of her.

Averie opened her thighs as wide as she possibly could. She reached and grabbed him down by his neck and bit into it so hard she lightly tore his skin. "Put yo dick in me right now, nigga, or kill me. I can't take this shit. I need you!" she cried.

Rayjon slammed it home and fell on top of her, trapped deep within her pussy. He raised his ass in the air and slammed it back home again. He slow stroked her juicy pussy but made sure she took all his meat. He found himself falling in love with that forbidden pussy.

Averie cried and moaned with her eyes closed. She felt him long stroking her and licking her tears away. Never before had she felt so healed, never had any man made the act of sex feel special.

"I told you I had you. I mean that shit," Rayjon growled, punching her kitty like a monster, while he sucked all over her neck. "Long as I'm alive you ain't needing fa' shit."

Chapter 14

Jersey held Jahni's hand as the little boy tried to keep up with her and Stacey. Stacey pushed the shopping cart inside of the parking lot, it was filled with groceries.

Around them, the snow fell in blankets. The wind picked up and nearly froze their faces. All Jersey wanted to do was get her grandson into her Land Rover, so she could go home and finish dinner. She had started the prep work for the baked lasagna, and she could taste it on her tongue.

Fishing her car key out of her pocket, she opened up the trunk of her truck, as Stacey guided the cart toward her, so they could start unloading the bags. As soon as the wind picked up its speed, Jersey wished she had paid one of the bag boys inside of the store to unload the groceries for them. It was too cold, and she didn't feel like helping at all. She opened the backdoor and helped Jahni into his booster seat.

Stacey tightened her hood around her head. The wind started to blow so hard she almost let out a few swear words. She was trying her best to maintain her composure when a black Escalade pulled behind her and didn't move. She was waiting on it to blow the horn or something, but it didn't. She turned around severely irritated and placed her hand on her hip, waiting about thirty more seconds in that position.

Finally, she got angry and threw her hands up, mugging the tinted windows. "Hey, what the fuck?"

"Lil' girl, watch your mouth around me," Jersey said, closing the back door to her truck. She then mugged the Cadillac SUV, too, and frowned.

All at once, all four doors opened and what seemed like eight men got out wearing white ski masks. Jersey nearly fell trying to run to the driver's side of her car. She had a .380 automatic under the seat that held eleven shots. She planned on using every bullet, too.

Stacey stood frozen in place. Every fiber in her being wanted to run, but for some reason she couldn't move. She watched one of the masked men walk up to her and slam their gun to her forehead. Then she heard thunder in the sky and the whole world turned red. She felt herself falling backward and the thunder boomed again and again.

Jersey watched as the man shot Stacey at point blank range in the face. The back of her head blew out, brain particles attacked the snow, turning it red, before melting it away altogether, and she landed on her side with blood pouring around her. The man stood over her and pulled the trigger again and again. She watched her body leap over and over on the ground. Fire sparked from his gun and wafted smoke into the air.

Jersey spun around, opened the driver's door and reached under the seat until three bullets slammed into her door.

Boom! Boom! Boom!

"Bitch, if you grab anything outta that car, I swear to God I'ma blow yo muthafuckin' head off. Get yo ass up and put your hands in the air."

Jersey slammed the clip into the gun and rocked it back.

Boom! Boom! Boom! Boom!

The bullets attacked the door and shattered the driver's side window. Jahni screamed at the top of his lungs.

Envy got pissed and took his mask off. "Fuck this! Jersey, this Envy! Get yo ass over here and drop that gun, hurry up! I ain't playing wit you and you already know how I get down!"

Jersey's heart started to beat faster after she heard Envy announce who he was. She saw him murder Stacey in her mind's eye and she knew he was up to absolutely no good. She wondered if somebody had given the order for her death.

"Jersey! Get the fuck over here!" He fired his .44 Bulldog and shattered her front windshield. Shooting through the car's open hatchback, an idea came to his head.

As fast as lightning, he shot into the car and yanked Jahni's entire booster seat and body out of the car while the little boy screamed at the top of his lungs. "Get up or I'm killing this lil' boy."

At learning that, she dropped the gun and slowly stood with her hands in front of her. "Envy, what the fuck you doin', man. Whatever you and my husband got going on that ain't got nothing to do with me and my grandbaby. Y'all got to keep that shit amongst men." She looked down at Stacey's body and couldn't believe the fate she'd met. She felt sorry for her but that was the risk one took when they became a part of The Edwards' family.

Envy bit Jahni on the cheek to make him scream. As soon as the little boy started screaming he slammed the .44 into his mouth. "If you don't get yo ass over here, I'm about to blow his shit back."

Envy held the boy in the air by his neck ready to blow out the back of his head.

***

Rayjon sucked his fingers tasting Averie's inner essence. He smiled running his fingers through her hair. He felt like million bucks. The best pussy he'd had in a long time and her thick thigh was still wrapped around him. He rubbed all over her ass, loving it.

"How you feel, lil' momma?"

Averie took a deep a breath and blew it out against his chest. She smelled the mixture of their sweaty sexes. She rubbed over his well-defined stomach muscles, then squeezed his dick.

"Amazing. You got my body tingling and pussy beyond sore. I told you to take it easy on me." She hit him playfully.

She kept quiet that slow love making did nothing for her. She needed him to hit it exactly like he had. She honestly had no gripes.

Rayjon laughed and gripped her ass. "All this shit need that thug-loving. You ain't equipped for no chump loving. Nigga get on this body, gotta put in work. Earn that stamp of approval, nah mean?"

She giggled. "I feel like giving your ass the biggest postage stamp at the post office. That thing that says certified." She stroked his dick up and down.

He smiled. "I just want you to know that I care about you beyond this sex shit. I mean don't get me wrong, I love every nook and cranny of this body. I could hit this shit all day, every day and never get tired of it. Word is bond." He opened her ass cheeks and stuck his middle finger in her hole.

She felt a little uneasy about his last statement. It wasn't that she didn't believe him, it was simply her insecurities getting the better of her all over again. "Rayjon, how do you know that you'll never get tired of it? I know it's plenty females out there that's about to be all over you. I'm pretty sure it ain't gon' be long before I'm old news. I just want you to always respect me." She paused, "And keep me under your gangsta wings."

Rayjon squeezed her booty. "I'll never get tired of you. What you got is my loyalty first, then my love and respect. Long as I don't go out here and wife nothing, you gon' always be priority. This world hard as a muthafucka for a black woman, especially when you coming from the bottom like you are. You need to be protected. You need for me to hold you down and buss that gun for you. Not just that, I gotta pave the way, so you can follow your dreams, whatever they may be. I wanna see you living the best and being your best possible self. Fuck them hoez out there. I got you." He hugged her tight, feeling her pussy scorch his thigh. He gripped her leg and pulled her all the way on top of him.

Averie looked into his eyes and felt her heart flutter. She didn't want to put a title to them to make things complicated. She didn't want to obligate him into doing anything. She just wanted whatever he was willing to render unto her. She leaned down and kissed his lips. Their kiss could be heard loudly in the room before she broke it off.

"Rayjon, I love you. I'll do anything for you. All I ask is that you treasure me and that you protect me from this cold, cold world because I need you. We ain't gotta put a title to this but I ain't fucking wit nobody but you. My loyalty belongs to you and so does my body. All I ask is that you continue to appreciate me in the ways you have. Please."

Rayjon looked into her eyes for a long time. He saw a wounded human being, one that was lost and barely hanging on. A female that needed pure love by any means and would accept anything just to get traces of it. He saw the longing for realness. A woman that needed to be protected and his heart felt some type of way for her.

He pulled her down and kissed her lips. "Every day I'm gon' find a new way to appreciate you and even if ever you feel like I'm slacking, I want you to call me out on my shit right away. You're in my heart and I got you. I pledge my loyalties to you one hunnit percent."

Those were all the words that Averie needed to hear, because she knew their family was huge on loyalty. As long as she knew he would be somewhere close in the picture, she felt she and Jahni would be okay.

She silently thanked Jehovah and with a smile kissed Rayjon's cheek while playing with the yellow diamond in his ear lobe.

***

"Snatch her ass up and if she move or do anything wrong, knock her head off her shoulders." He ordered as his two little homies yanked Jersey from the concrete violently and slapped a piece of duct tape around her mouth, before tossing her on the floor of the Escalade.

Fifteen minutes later, they were in the basement of one of his traps. Jersey was duct taped to a chair along with Jahni, who had his hands cuffed behind his back.

Envy paced back and forth in front of her constantly sniffing snot back into his nose. Four men stood along the wall of the basement with half masks, that covered their faces from the nose down.

Envy walked over to her and ripped the duct tape off her face. He watched her wince in pain with her eyes closed and he couldn't help smiling. There was still an utter disdain inside of him for her, all because of Greed. He felt she chose Greed over him and ever since that she treated him like shit. That made him angry, although low-key he still had a thing for her. A thing he couldn't quite put his finger on.

Jersey took a deep breath and exhaled. Her nose had been stopped up horribly, so it was hard for her to breathe when her mouth was duct taped. She thought she was going to die from suffocation. Her heart had never pounded harder in her chest.

"Envy, why am I down here? Why did you kill Stacey?" she screamed, becoming angry. A line of snot leaked onto her upper lip, and she tried to sniff it back up but the cold she had wouldn't allow her to.

Envy stopped pacing and stood in front of her. He mugged her for a long time, then side-stepped, upped a .40 caliber and pointed it at Jahni.

Boom! Boom! Boom! Boom! Boom! Boom!

The fire spit from his gun, knocking her grandson backward before the bullets ate at his flesh.

Jahni saw Envy standing over him and it made him want to run to his grandmother, but he feared getting in trouble. His hands hurt from the cuffs Envy had tightly placed around them.

Envy pointed his gun at him and pulled the trigger four times, knocking his brains out the back of his head, causing blood to splatter all over the room.

"Ahh! What have you done? What have you done?" Jersey wailed, looking at the body of her slain four-year-old grandson.

Her heart split in two. He was her only one and she loved him with all her heart. She tried to give him the world. Out of everything she had given, the one thing he needed most was her protection and she had failed him miserably. She cried so hard that her entire body got weak. She smelled his blood in the air along with the gunpowder and his blood pooled around him. His eyes were wide open but unseeing.

After killing Jahni, Envy felt his high going away. He started to feel sick. He sat on the floor Indian style and tied the belt around his arm before shooting up with heroin. As soon as it hit his blood stream, he felt cool as a fan.

"Your punk ass husband told me that I had a week to leave this city." His head rolled around on his shoulders and he nodded out for a full minute.

"What the fuck that got to do with those kids you killed or me for that matter?" Jersey screamed once her impatience kicked in.

Envy jerked awake and stood. "Bitch, it's war! You know how your husband get down, and so do I. Now I ain't going no muthafucking where and since I ain't, that mean it's about to be a whole lot of bloodshed. I'm to the point that I don't give a fuck. If it's war your nigga want, that's what he gone get."

Jersey spit at his feet. "Nigga, you ain't nothing but a muthafucking coward. You picking on women and children, that don't make you no killa. That makes you a straight bitch!"

Envy reached and slapped her so hard it sounded like thunder in the room. Her neck slightly popped. She yelped in pain and all the noises gave him a hard on.

"Ain't Greed taught you no manners in all these years?" He snorted and hocked a yellow loogy at her feet.

Jersey's face felt like it had been burned with acid. Tears ran down her cheeks and her entire body started to shake.

"Now yo husband started all this by fucking wit Lily. The nigga had the nerves to strap bombs across her chest and bring her to me." He laughed. "What, I wasn't supposed to do nothing about that, just 'pose to sit back and let big, bad ass Greed fuck over my wife and not do nothing to his, huh?" He slapped her across the face twice as hard this time. "Bitch you got me fucked me up."

Jersey spit blood across the brick wall. She felt her teeth stick into her jaw and her lips swelled up like she had gotten stung by a bee. Envy grabbed a handful of her hair and yanked her head backward, roughly.

"Bet you wish you would have chosen me over that nigga now, don't you? Bet I seem like the muthafuckin' president all the sudden, huh? Answer me, now!" He slapped her again so hard that he knocked her out.

***

"That ain't like yo momma to not her answer her phone, especially when I told her I was gon' call at this time." Averie said, slipping into her jogging pants.

Rayjon frowned. "Ain't none of the family saying they know where she at either. My old man down in Miami on business. He'll be back in the morning. What about Stacey? You hit her up?" he asked, getting dressed.

"Nall, first I was trying to see if she was up and on Facebook, but she ain't. Aiight, I'm finna call Stacey phone right now."

Rayjon put the .40 Glock on his waist and fixed his vest in place, before slipping his Ferragamo over it. He was starting to get a little nervous because he knew how his mother got down. She always answered her phone, even if something had happened to her phone she would always let someone in the family know. He couldn't help feeling in his gut that something wasn't right.

T.J. Edwards

Chapter 15

"Yeah, yeah, nigga, hit yo ass wit that Bodak Yellow. Oww," Dior said before turning around and popping her ass in front of Ajani. She had on a Roberto Cavalli dress that hugged her ass so right that he found himself salivating. Her ass rippled and shook as the dress rose on her hips.

Ajani reached and threw twenty gees against her back. "I don't give a fuck who you is now. I knew you from the projects and I'm trying to get you to keep shit gangsta and let me hit this pussy. Money still make the muthafuckin' world go round, right?"

Dior squatted down, fell forward and made her ass clap. She slowly pulled her dress up until her entire ass was exposed. The lime-green G-string separated her globes. She felt Ajani rubbing between her cheeks and rocked her thighs further apart.

"You ain't gotta bring up my past, Papi. We can handle business in this bitch without getting all personal." She looked at him over her shoulders, licking her lips. "How much you just throw at me?"

She could tell it was all hundreds scattered across the strip club's office. Just by eye, she added up over fifteen thousand dollars.

"That's twenty bands and all I wanna see is you buss that muthafucka open. Then ride this dick like yo life depending on it. Word is bond, fuck me hunnit by hunnit."

Dior smiled showing off her new grill.

Less than a year ago she couldn't get a nigga to throw a hundred-dollar bill at her. After a few mixtapes, niggas was trying to eat her shit for breakfast and offer her the world.

"Eww, that sound good to me, Papi. Ain't no thang. We all in the life, right?"

Ajani wasn't trying to hear none of that, he pushed her down to her knees and pulled his dick out. "Handle yo business."

***

Greed watched Aiden pick the fat white man up by his throat and carry him to the bottom quarters of the yacht, while August held the pistol to the other man slowly walking him to the same destination. They were the last two names on the hit list and Greed wanted to fulfill the contract, so he could get on with his life. The worst feeling in the world to him was owing somebody. He could never think straight when he owed other people, so he had to finalize the contract.

Aiden waited for Greed to walk through the door before closing it behind him. The sun was shining bright, with a cool breeze coming off the water. He smelled the salt water in the air and wrinkled his nose. When he turned around, he saw Greed lean back and punch the fat man straight in the nose, his blood spurted across his fist. Aiden saw that the man's nose was bent way too far to the right, obviously broken.

Mitchell felt the blow and then heard a loud snap. He eyes watered and it felt like somebody jammed a screw driver in his face.

"Argghh! Shit! What's all this about?" he bellowed in anger. He had paid back the million-dollar loan he had taken out with Fat Charlie. He hoped the man didn't call for his death now that he had received all of the payments.

Scott felt blow after blow slam against his face. They came so fast he couldn't keep up with them and the pain was horrible. His heart pounded so hard in his chest he feared his pace maker would stop working. He wondered why they were being attacked. His messy divorce crossed his mind and he wondered if his wife had put a hit out on him.

Greed grabbed Mitchell by his thin hair and glared into his face with hatred, while August sat the laptop up and Kabir's face appeared.

"Payback is a bitch, Mitchell. What did I tell you would happen if you ever tried to screw me over? What did I promise you, if you betrayed me?" he hissed with venom.

Mitchell swallowed and let out a yelp as felt Greed tighten his grip on his hair. The weight caused his neck to become stiff.

"Kabir, my hands were tied, I did all I could, honest. I never forgot you, me and Scott been trying to figure out things for the greater good of you. Tell him, Scott."

Scott's face was mangled, blood poured from it and his nose was broken. He felt in his gut that of this had something to do with Mitchell. Once again, the man involved him in some bullshit.

First, the loans he had taken out in his name and credit with Fat Charlie and now the double-crossing of Kabir. He wanted no parts of it.

He took a deep breath. "Don't put me in your shit. You fucked up the paperwork. You got sloppy and Homeland Security got wind of it because of your negligence. Not me."

Mitchell passed gas again as his stomach turned upside down and he wanted to throw up. It seemed like the world was spinning fast and he couldn't slow it down. He thought about crying or even begging for mercy.

"Son of a bitch! I'm not dying for you. Whatever you, did fix it. You leave me out of this and handle your business as a man."

Aiden slid the blade out of his sleeve and curled his upper lip in annoyance. He hated when friends flipped on each other. He felt as if the two buddies did dirt together, then they should ride it out in loyalty until the bitter end. When the end came they should face it together.

Kabir shook his head. "You jeopardized the whole mission, and both of you put my family at risk. Lives were lost, and land was stolen. With you alive, the fight for my life is impossible, so you have to go. Pay your debt to me." he nodded at Greed. "End them and this makes us even."

Greed took Mitchell by the head and with all his might yanked it backwards, which caused his neck to snap in two. The sound of it breaking was so loud that August winced in fascination.

"Holy fuck, man!" Scott emptied his entire bladder on himself. The piss saturated his pants and ran down his legs. He looked over and saw how Mitchell's head was snapped all the way backward and he started crying. "Please, I don't wanna die. I've worked so hard to do right by everybody. I'm so sorry, Kabir. I didn't have anything to do with how they screwed you over. I…"

Aiden stepped forward and put his fingers in the man's mouth, some on the upper row of teeth and some on the bottom row. With all his might he started to pull them away, separately. He was tired of all the fucking whining.

Scott felt pressure being applied, then his jaw popped and then the pain started. A cracking of his bones resonated in his ear. He felt his jaw shattering and breaking apart on both sides. It felt as if his face was caving in and the pain shot all over.

Beads of sweat appeared under Aiden's mask as he continued to pull apart the man's mouth with all his might. He heard the sound of twigs being stepped on in the woods, then he felt his bones gave way. He hollered out loud.

Snap! Crack!

Scott's mouth was ripped in two separate directions. The pain was unbearable. He prayed for death. He screamed at the top of his lungs and it sounded muffled. A bunch of noise coming out a bloody hole.

August looked intrigued because he had never seen a man's face do that before. He knew it was something that he would have to try one day. He loved his big brother so much that he idolized him.

Aiden took the blade and cut Scott's throat back and forth, then pulled his head backward and watched him bleed out.

***

"Are you sure that's the vehicle you saw driving away from the scene?"

The fat man nodded his head and adjusted his glasses on his nose. "Clean as day. It was an all-black Cadillac Escalade. The dude had a mask on, but they didn't cover his long dreadlocks." He shook his head. "Sad too, the way he emptied that gun into that girl. He ain't have to do all that. He could have killed the other one, too, but he threw her in the truck. Had the nerve to choke the child, holding him in the air and everything." He adjusted his glasses once again.

Rayjon stuffed a hundred-dollar bill in his hand and made him ball up his fist. "Thank you, sir, I appreciate the information."

Perry waved him off. "It ain't nothing. I seen what I saw and I'm telling you what I did. Now you betta be careful because that man is crazy. Shooting people all willy nilly and thangs. Best you go to the police and save face. Too young to die. I…"

Rayjon brushed past him and hopped in his Range Rover. Averie sat in the passenger seat with her hands covering her face. He heard her whimpering and rubbed her back.

"It's Envy. That nigga got my mom's and Jahni. We finna have to tear this city up to get them back. That fool just as crazy as my pops. I know when he find out he finna go ballistic. I gotta drop you off at home as much as I hate to, but it ain't safe for you to be in these streets right now."

Averie took a deep breath. "Why is he doing this? Why is he attacking our family? I thought he was your father's brother? Help me to understand what is going on."

Rayjon pulled out the parking lot. The snow was coming down so bad that he could barely see. "That nigga got a sick obsession with my mother and he just mad because my father took her a long time ago back when they were kids. My old man pulled a seven-year bid back in the day when I was like two or three years old. Envy pretty much held her down until he came home. But as soon as my Pops did get home she pretty much kicked Envy to the curb and never really fucked with him on any level, not even as family. I guess that nigga taking offense to that."

Rayjon pulled into traffic and had to blow his horn to alert a tow truck that almost smashed into him.

Averie braced herself and snapped her seatbelt around her. She needed to hear more of the story, so she could get an understanding as to what was taking place. "So, is he just jealous of your father? And if so, do you think it's to the point that he would kill your mother and Jahni?" Her voice broke up.

Rayjon shrugged his shoulders. "If that nigga bodied Stacey like that and put all them holes in my mother's truck door, then ain't no telling what he'll do. We just gotta get to her before he do some shit like that." Rayjon picked his phone and called Ajani to let him know what had gone down, but got no answer after a few rings.

***

Ajani pulled out of Dior's pussy as he fed her his dick. He watched as she sucked her own juices off, before sucking his balls. She was a monster and he had plans to get her and Vanity in the same bed.

His phone vibrated on his desk, but he ignored it. "Let me fuck that ass one time, ma."

Dior smiled and kissed his dickhead before assuming the position.

***

Envy raised his foot and brought it down hard stomping Jahni's dead head, causing it to squirt more brain matter. He kicked it and proceeded to stomp over and over again with his Timb's.

"Stop it! Stop it! Stop it!" Jersey was in tears. "What's the matter with you?" She raised her foot as three big rats surrounded her chair and sniffed upward at her with their big, red beady racoon eyes.

Envy kicked the dead baby against the wall and nearly slipped on his blood. Jahni's body landed upside sown and more blood poured from his body. Envy hated the little boy, hated him because he reminded him of what Jersey had stripped him of.

Jersey took a deep breath. Her face stung and her left eye was swollen shut. "Why, Envy? Why? Why? Why?" She sobbed, barely above a whisper. It was like her soul had slipped through her fingers as she laid eyes on her grandson's lifeless body. "I want him back, Envy! Bring him back!" She hollered her request, knowing that it was an impossible task.

Envy frowned. "Why couldn't you just allow me to be a part of his life? Why did you turn your back on me when he came home after all we had been through in those seven years?" he asked this question through clenched teeth.

Jahni's body slowly fell on its side, his neck bent awkwardly. Very slowly rats creeped over to him and started feasting on his body. Gnawing away like he was the best meal of their lives.

Jersey closed her eyes, her first grandchild. Hot torrents of grief coursed down her face. She could not comprehend what was happening.

"I didn't allow you in his life because you weren't worthy of him. All you cared about was that fucking dope, chasing disease ridden women and the streets. You ain't got one ounce of compassion in your heart for nobody. All you care about is you. Your genes are already too strong in my son. The last thing he needed was your constant presence." she spat at him with look of disgust.

Envy felt like a knife was stabbed in his heart. Although he guessed she felt some type of way about him, he never thought that she hated him so much. Her answer to his questions had told him everything he needed to know.

He grew angry. "But he's my muthafuckin' son. When Greed went down I steeped in and treated yo ass like royalty. You ain't have to pay a bill or lift a muthafuckin' finger. Yet you repaid me by shitting on me as soon as that nigga came home."

"You killed your own fucking grandchild, you sick son of a bitch! Jahni is dead, all because of you. You think I wanted my son to grow up with you as his father and it's not even guaranteed that you are his father. We fucked one time. One time in a moment of weakness. That doesn't mean that you are Ajani's father!" she screamed.

He had her mind so scrambled. There she was at first speaking as if Jahni wasn't his grandchild, when the truth of the matter was that she really didn't know for certain. After Greed had been locked away, she and him were still sleeping together on conjugal visits. Around the same time when Jersey's father had passed away, Greed was in segregation and she was unable to visit in any way for two entire weeks.

Envy had consoled her being an absolute gentleman attending to her every need and she made a mistake.

The following week, Greed was let off lock down and they were in sack screwing like rabbits and he began the process of healing her in ways that only he could. No one could do her like Greed.

The night with Envy had been a major disappointment and she still felt sick. As a woman, she stood on her gangsta and told Greed how everything went down between them word for word, not even leaving out the part about Envy's little dick.

Envy stood in front of her and blinked tears. "Bitch, don't you know that I love you? That I will always love you and if you ain't with me I ain't finna allow you to be wit nobody else?" He grabbed a handful of her hair and put his face so close to hers that he could smell her perfume and sweat. "What that nigga got that I ain't, huh? Why you love his bitch ass so much?"

Jersey had visions of killing him every time he disrespected the love of her life. She thought about torturing him and watching him bleed out slowly. She would do the murder all on her own, making sure that it lasted at least an hour. Then she would cook a full course meal in celebration of his demise.

"Answer me, bitch." He licked her face from the chin all the way up to her hairline, tasting the sweat and relishing in its salty flavor. The taste reminded him of how good her pussy was on his tongue. He remembered her being a squirter and that made him smile.

Jersey tried to head butt him. "My husband is a muthafuckin' G and you are a bitch!" She yanked her head forward after he released her. "You think you tough, fuck nigga? You think you gon' get away with this shit when you already know how we get down on this side of the DNA! Punk, even if Ajani was yours, my husband takin' him from you!" She spat at his feet. "Ajani gon' kill you when he finds out wat you've done. I know my men tearing this city up lookin' for me, so you can kill me, but when you finish, just know you gon' be next."

After hearing all of that, something in Envy snapped and he decided he was going to make her pay.

Chapter 16

Whoom! Whoom!
"Kick that bitch one more time!"
Whoom! Kack-kack-kack-kack!
The door flew in after the last kick by Aiden. As soon as it flew inward, he took the .45 out of the small of his back.

Lily dropped the strainer of macaroni. It fell to the floor and popped up burning her on the ankles. Her eyes were as big as saucers. The noise in the front of the house told her one thing, that she was under attack either by the Feds or by someone from Envy's street life.

Her heart pounded in her chest as she tried to figure out what to do. She considered running out the back door, but her car was in the front of the house. She prayed it was the police and not a robber or even worse.

Thoughts of being snatched up by the yellow man nearly made her hysterical. Before she could settle on what to do, Ajani was in the kitchen pointing a shotgun at her chest. Behind him was Greed, the yellow man, Rayjon and August.

Ajani frowned and took the shotgun, slamming the barrel into her chest so hard that he broke four of her ribs.
Chik! Chik!
He pumped it. "Bitch, where that nigga Envy at and be smart because I'm all out of patience."

The rest of them spread out and got to kicking in doors, flipping mattresses and nearly everything in sight. Greed came back into the kitchen and narrowed his eyes into slits.

Lily shit on herself, diarrhea type shit. It slid down the back of her leg like brown oatmeal with smoke coming from it. The smell was horrendous. Enough to make the average person sick on the stomach, but not them. No, that type of fear told them that they were in full control.

"Arrghh! Please don't shoot!" Karissa screamed from the other room.

Lily heard her daughter's pleas and sank down to her knees. Now she was wishing she had allowed her to spend the night at her cousin's house, but Envy had put a stop to it, saying he didn't trust her side of the family around his daughter. Had she listened, their daughter would have been safe and sound and not being dragged across the floor by her hair.

August threw the girl against the stove and put the .45 to her head. He watched as Rayjon threw the boy that had been hiding under her bed into the refrigerator so hard that all of the boxes of cereal fell on top of him, before busting onto the floor.

Ajani jammed the barrel of the shotgun to Lily's neck and lowered his eyes. "I'ma ask you one more time Lily, where the fuck is your husband at? I know that nigga said something to you! Now he got my mother on some fuck shit. Tell me what's good."

Lily screamed as she felt the barrel of the shotgun being slammed into the back of her head. At hearing Envy's name, she felt sick. She should have known that all of this had something to do with him.

"Ajani, I swear I don't know. He doesn't tell me anything. I never question him ab…"

Before she could finish, she heard a loud boom. She saw the fire leave the barrel and the next thing she remembered was the feeling of her head exploding.

"Ahhh! Ajani! Mommy!" Karissa screamed and tried to jump from the floor, but August pushed her back down aggressively.

She watched Ajani blow her mother's head clean off her shoulders. It exploded as if she had swallowed a stick of dynamite. Blood was splattered all around the kitchen as if they had been having a red paint fight.

Greed watched Lily's headless body fall on its side. He smelled the gunpowder and blood in the air. He never had a problem with the woman, he always found her to be respectful and kind. She had a good heart, but in his mind, she had married the wrong dude. He shrugged his shoulders and knelt in front of Karissa. The little girl's face was as red as a strawberry. She cried so hard as she could with her chest heaving up and down.

"Karissa, where is your father? Did he say anything to you?"

Karissa was crying so hard she couldn't breathe. Her mother was dead, no longer living. She was having a hard time processing it. What would she do now? Who would take care of her? Where would she live? Would she be forced to stay with her father? Would he beat her like he always did, but even more so now that her mother was dead?

"Karissa! Where is your father?" Greed hollered, losing his patience. He knew that time of the essence. The longer they played around, the less chance his wife and grandson had on being alive.

She shook her head. "I, I, I, don't know where my father is." Snot ran out of her nose, her yellow face covered in tears. "I haven't seen him since yesterday morning, before I went to school."

Ajani stepped in front of her with the shotgun ready to blow her head off like he did with her mother. As far as he was concerned, she was the enemy and he didn't give a fuck about blowing her shit back. He pumped the shotgun. "Bitch, tell me where he at right now!"

Karissa whimpered and covered her face with her hands. She was so scared, she didn't want to die. She was only eleven years old, as of three weeks ago.

Boom! Click! Click! Boom!

The fire lit up the kitchen. Karissa flew back and landed against the refrigerator, with half of her face missing. It looked like a tiger had gotten a hold of her and tried to devour her entire left side of her face.

Ajani got tired of all the fucking crying and whimpering. He imagined his mother was somewhere doing the same thing and that pissed him off. He didn't give a fuck how old the girl was.

The fact of the matter was she had already seen all their faces, so she was going to be killed anyway. He learned a long time ago that when it came down to killing, he had to set all of his sentimental emotions aside. He had to look at every victim as a dangerous enemy, nothing else.

Chucky pissed himself. He was becoming hysterical. He started wheezing with his asthma getting the better of him. He couldn't breathe. He tried to remember where he'd left his inhaler, but with everything going on around him, he couldn't even think straight.

His chest started to burn, and it felt like he was swallowing boiling hot water and his lungs were on fire. He tried to stand up, but Aiden punched him in the chest so hard he flew from his feet and landed in the pantry.

Now he really couldn't breathe. He struggled to catch his breath, wheezing louder and louder, then panic set in. Hysteria was getting the best of him. The acid feeling in his chest started to get worse and he felt his lungs swelling up.

He stood up again and Aiden kicked him directly in the chest, knocking the wind out of him.

He landed on his back fighting to stay alive, chest rising, huffing, puffing, coughing and wheezing. It felt like his entire chest was on the verge of exploding. The world started to spin, it got fuzzy and he had thoughts of his head being held under water. There was a loud ringing in his ears, then poof! His heart burst and his lungs collapsed as he flopped around on the floor.

Aiden bent down and checked his pulse before wrapping his big hands around his neck and choking him for another three minutes.

T.J. Edwards

Chapter 17

Envy grabbed a handful of Jersey's hair and yanked her head backwards as she laid in the bed, flat on her stomach. "Get yo ass up and eat this food. I'm not gon' tell you again." He pushed her face back to the mattress and stood up, taking the plate of scrambled eggs and waffles, throwing them on to her back.

She felt the food land on her and refused to move. She was so weak and hadn't eaten in three days, her throat hurt, and she was dizzy. Anytime she smelled the aroma of food, it made her sick. She missed her family and wondered when they'd be coming for her. She refused to allow herself to think they weren't coming. No! She knew her men way better than that, especially her husband.

"Get yo ass up and eat or I'ma finna beat you until you piss out blood. I'm tired of playin' these mafuckin' games with you, now get up!" He pulled his belt from around his waist, whipped it through the air and brought it down full speed, making contact with her naked back.

The belt collided with her back. "Ahhhhh!" The pain was so unbearable, yet she barely moved. She blinked tears and thought about her family. She felt so lost that the pain didn't even register. She missed them so bad.

Envy raise the belt again and slashed her nearly in the same spot. He knew he was going to have to whip her into shape. Greed had taught her too well. He'd raised her to be a monster like him.

The previous night he'd tried to get on top of her, but she fought him for so long he'd lost his erection. He also had a black eye from one of her punches that landed.

Jersey clenched her jaw and absorbed the pain from the lashes. She didn't allow them to conquer her body. Greed told her a long time ago that pain was ninety percent mental and only ten percent physical. If she could focus on other things while she endured the pain, she could conquer it and it would never harm her. So, she thought about him, Ajani and Rayjon.

Envy went crazy. Whipping and beating her back again and again. He switched hands with the belt and kept on going until sweat was dripping from his face.

The belt slashed Jersey's neck, but she was in a faraway land on a cruise with Greed drinking Merlot while he held her firmly in his big massive arms, kissing her all over the back of her neck with his juicy lips.

She missed his big dimples and his smooth bald head that drove her crazy.

He would kill a million niggas for her with no remorse. She'd watched him in action time and time again. He was a real gangsta, the kind that stood tall on his *G*.

Envy swung the belt one final time and his arm went completely out. He watched the blood seep out of the welts on her back. Her lips were moving as if she was talking to herself.

He dropped the belt and pulled her by the ankle until she landed on the floor by his feet. He wrapped his fingers into her hair and slapped her across the face.

"Bitch, listen to me! Can't you see that I care about you?" He slapped her again and threw her onto her back before straddling her. He ripped her bra from her body, causing her small brown breasts to expose themselves. The visual excited him immediately.

The smacks brought Jersey back to reality. She looked up into Envy's menacing face as he ripped her bra away from her body and squeezed her breasts, pushing them together, leaning down attempting to put her left nipple in his mouth. She snapped!

Pumping her hips upward she tried to buck him off her. When that didn't work, she felt him pull on both of her nipples roughly before twisting them. The pain attacked her right away.

"Get off me you fuckin' rapist!" She wished that she were stronger. *Why did God have to make men more physically stronger than women? Didn't he know that they would use that imbalance of power to their advantage?* she thought.

Envy laughed. He knew she would not have enough strength to get him off her especially since she hadn't eaten anything.

He was tired of playing games. He wanted to be knee-deep inside of her pussy for old times' sake. He only gotten the chance to fuck her one time and though he enjoyed it, he felt he didn't last long enough. This time he would savor the moment. He would enjoy every stroke until he spilled his seed deep in her belly. He would fuck her so good she would forget all about Greed. He would stay on her brain from then on out. He licked her thick nipple and placed his thigh between her legs.

Jersey could smell his funky body and it was making her sick. He smelled like ass and musk. He needed to wash his ass badly and brush his teeth.

When she felt his filthy tongue on her nipple, she nearly threw up right in his face. The first thing she thought about was betraying Greed by allowing another nigga to touch her in any way. She felt the tears coming out her eyes and Greed's voice invading her brain. *"Baby girl, you never let no nigga invade my temple. This body belongs to me. As a woman of loyalty, you devote every portion, nook and cranny of it to me, your husband until the death. You die before you ever let a nigga defile you."* She squeezed her eyelids together.

Envy yanked her panties away and forced his thick fingers into her lips separating them and playing around the hole. His dick was harder than it had ever been. He imagined himself sliding into her fat pussy again and he started to shake.

Jersey had the best pussy he had ever came across. Not only was it hotter than lava, but it had been tight and wet the entire time. He was obsessed with her slim figure and bubble ass. Though she was nearing forty, she didn't look older than twenty-one. That ageless beauty drove him crazy. The aspect of rape caused him to salivate at the mouth. He took his shirt off and threw it against the wall as he continued to massage her sex lips.

Tears poured out of Jersey's eyes. She prayed that God would get to her in time before Envy fully violated her. She would rather die than to have him enter her body. Her temple belonged to Greed. It had since the beginning. He had given her the world and never did anything to hurt her. She had always been first in his life. Then came their children. His loyalty was endless and without fault.

She shook her head from right to left. *"Fight, baby girl."* She imagined what Greed would say and that's what she decided to do.

Just as Envy leaned over to suck on Jersey's neck, he felt her knee slam into his balls once, then again. He saw himself falling forward, then she was locking onto his face with her teeth and he could hear her growling as if she were a pit-bull. She shook from side to side and he could feel his cheek leaving away from the bone.

"Harrr! Harrr! Harrr!" Jersey growled, biting and yanking on his face with her teeth.

She felt his blood spurt into her mouth and that excited her. She kneed him in the nuts again and he yelped as if he was a straight whiney bitch.

Envy started to scream when she brought her knee up and crashed it into his sack again. His balls went into his stomach and stayed there. He threw up all over himself and her, then she spit his cheek on to the floor and attacked his face again, biting like a vicious rabid animal.

"Kill that bitch nigga, baby girl! That's my muthafuckin' temple. You die before you let a nigga defile you! Kill! Kill! Kill! Kill! You die before you let a nigga defile you! Fight! Kill! Fight! Loyalty! Loyalty! Loyalty!" She heard Greed's voice in her head and it made her go crazy.

She bit into Envy's neck and punctured his jugular. Blood spurted and ran down her chin. She took her mouth away to lick her lips before attacking another vein and ripping it to shreds! He bucked on the floor, bleeding profusely with his eyes rolling into the back of his head.

She straddled him, looking down and smiling. "I belong to Greed, bitch nigga! You can't control a Queen like me. I hate yo type of nigga!"

She bit into his face again and pulled away a huge chunk of it. She chewed it for a few seconds, tasting the rubber like skin before spitting it into his face in anger.

Envy could not move. He felt weak and woozy. His blood spurt from so many different places that he didn't know what to do.

He saw Jersey standing looking down at him with an evil smile on her face. His blood was all over her mouth and nose. She looked like she just ate a bowl of tomato soup without using a spoon. Her small titties jiggled slightly as her chest heaved up and down. He wished he had left her alone, and that he hadn't sent his security away from that particular trap, so he could rape her. He never knew how psychotic she was.

Jersey turned her head to the side with blood dripping from her chin. She looked down on him and her hatred started to come to the forefront all over again.

She took the ashtray from the dresser and threw it into the mirror that was on the back of the door. The glass shattered into twenty big pieces. She took the pillow off the bed and removed the burgundy pillowcase, before wrapping it around one of the big shards of glass.

She knelt on the side of Envy and curled her upper lip. *"Kill that bitch nigga, baby girl! Body that punk! Do that shit fa daddy! You belong to me. You know how we get down!"* she heard Greed's voice in her head again.

"Arrrgghh! Ahhhh! Arrrghhh! Shit!" Envy hollered as he felt jersey dragging the shard of glass into the middle of his neck and pulling downward, splitting him open.

She would start and stop. Then she raised it above her head and stabbed it into him all over again dragging it down, ripping him wide open until his insides were oozing out of his ribcage. She took her fingers and bust his wound open, pulling him all the way apart.

Jersey smiled. She punched her fist into the hole in his stomach and felt around. It felt hot and squishy just like Greed told her it did. She took her hand out and grabbed the glass stabbing downward again and again while blood popped up and decorated the room.

She was lost and in a zone. Stabbing an entire hour after Envy had already been dead.

Chapter 18

Greed kicked in the door to the bedroom and found Jersey still on her knees stabbing Envy like crazy. Even after he knelt at her side and wrapped his arms around her she continued to stab him repeatedly. Blood popped upward and landed all over his face and neck. Jersey looked like she'd been sprayed with his blood by a water gun.

She cried and mumbled under her breath. Greed felt the tears leave his eyes. He was silently praying his wife hadn't snapped, praying that she didn't have a nervous breakdown and that Envy had not gotten the chance to sexually violate his temple.

He bear hugged her and kissed her soft, yet bloody cheek. "Baby girl, baby girl, calm down. I'm here now, ma. You're safe. You ain't gotta worry about this fuck nigga no more."

Jersey's body shook as she was miles away from reality. In her mind, she was only imagining Greed being there. His voice was not real. It was just a guide just like it had always been when she was away from him and needed strength. She wished he really was there because she needed him so fucking bad. She needed him to protect her from Envy before he woke back up and tried to attack her again. She didn't want to fight anymore, she wanted to go and make Sunday dinner, everybody had to be hungry by now she figured.

Greed kissed her again. Now tears were really coming down his cheeks. He was starting to panic. He couldn't live with the fact that Jersey would have gone insane all because he wasn't there to protect her, that she had to mentally escape her attacker while he did God only knows what to her. He wouldn't be able to go on in life knowing he had failed her. She had been his everything ever since he understood what love really meant.

He squeezed her tighter. "Jersey, please, snap out that shit, ma. I need you, baby girl. I need you to come back to me."

Tears left Jersey's eyes. She needed Greed so bad. His voice was making the longing for him worse. She knew he would be there to save her soon from the animal of Envy before he went inside of her body and defiled her in a way she would never be able to live with. She was sure that Greed would be on his way soon.

Greed didn't know what to do. He squeezed her with all his might and shook his head. Finally, he felt he would try one last thing. It was the only thing that he could think that should work.

He sat on the floor and pulled her into his embrace, stroking her long hair, while rubbing her back. He rocked her in his arms as if she were a little child and in his mind, in that moment, she was.

He cleared his throat and prepared for the lyrics. *"You have given me the best of you. And you have made my dreams come true. And after all the things you have done. Girl, it makes me say that you are more than a woman, so I'm...Dedicating this one to my favorite girl. She's the only woman in the whole wide world..."*

Jersey jerked violently, and her eyes shot wide open as tears flowed down her cheeks. She frowned, then started smiling with her eyes closed while she allowed herself to be rocked back and forth.

The lyrics to R. Kelly's song, *Favorite Girl*, snapped her out of her zone and released her back into the realm of him. The song soothed her soul as she allowed for them to take her on a journey, in which he was the captain of the ship.

Then all at once she remembered Jahni and she shot up from the floor. "He killed our grandson! He killed Stacey and he tried to rape me!" Her chest heaved up and down.

Greed got up and placed a sheet around her to cover her naked upper half. "Where did he leave Jahni's body?" he asked clenching his jaw before looking down on to Envy with obvious hatred. His body looked like an autopsy had been performed on it.

Jersey shrugged her shoulders. "I don't know, baby, but he's dead. Our first grandchild is dead and it's all because of that sick son of a bitch. Ahhh!" She dropped to her knees and started to punch Envy's dead head again and again, imagining him killing Jahni.

Chapter 19

"That's how it has to go. There is absolutely no way around it. I want you to murder him, then take care of his entire crew and I need this done before the month is out." Kabir said, looking directly into King's eyes.

There wasn't any other American that he trusted more than him. King had a reputation that proceeded him all the way to the Middle East.

King clenched his jaw. There was no doubt in his mind that he was up for the task. Kabir had pulled enough strings to get him released, now he was asking him to pay up his side of the debt. He wanted Greed and his entire crew murdered. The entire job could not take longer than thirty days' time, either.

Kabir leaned into his ear. "The bounty is five million dollars if you can complete the task in less than thirty days. If you can do it before then, you'll get ten. You have two point five that has already been made available to you. The end of his life is very important to me and a few more higher ups. You take care of this the right way and The Underworld will be placed at your feet. He is an animal, so you'll have to be relentless. You were looking for a way into ISIS, well here is your key."

King clenched his jaw and slowly nodded his head, he had heard a lot about the infamous Greed. They were no strangers to each other. Greed operated out of the East coast and King was strongly in the Midwest. Deeply rooted in the city of Chicago, Illinois, where he was a living street legend.

He decided that he would use this green light to not only take out Greed and his entire organization, but also a strong hold of the East coast. Then for him all that would be left was the South and Big Meech. He curled his lip at the thought of him. Yeah, he would fulfill the contract on Greed immediately.

***

Three more days passed by before they were able to have Stacey's funeral. It was a windy and very snowy day. The mood for the entire family was down. All having heavy hearts for the woman coupled with the loss of Jahni. The service lasted two hours. Averie's family had flown from all around the country just to be present. When it was all said and done many hugs had been given and numerous tears shed.

Ajani had had enough of all the mushy shit. He felt like he needed a break from it all, so he tapped Vanity on the thigh. She gave him a crazy look. "I need for you to move a lil' bit, so that I can get out of this church. I need some air."

Vanity squeezed his hand in understanding. She stood up, so he could get out of the section they were sitting in inside the church. She hugged him and kissed his cheek. "Don't worry about it, baby. Tonight, me and Dior gon' do whatever it takes to make you feel all better. Whatever you want, you gon' get. I promise. You hear me?" she kissed his cheek again, her perfume wafting up his nose.

Even though they were at a funeral, Ajani still found himself getting excited while imagining what he was gon' have them do.

He hugged her and made his way outside of the church. He took a fat blunt from inside of his coat pocket and opened the doors to the church.

As soon as he did, his eyes got as big as paper plates. The last thing he remembered was wishing that he'd put on his bulletproof vest that morning before the rapid shots spit down on him.

***

Rayjon heard all the gunfire and pushed Averie to the floor before pulling his twin .45's out of their holsters. He could hear the sounds of people dropping to the floor, along with screams of panic. They were under attack by what sounded like an entire fucking army.

***

Greed made Jersey get down and slammed the magazines into his Glock .40s. His heart was beating loudly in his chest, his eye scanning the entire church as the windows shattered and bullets flew inside and chopped up the wooden pews. There was a loud boom. Then the church was on fire with people running around engulfed. He had to figure out the attack. They were coming at him hard.

***

King sent ten more men to the back of the church after giving them the order to go in and kill everybody in sight.

He took the grenade out of the bag and squeezed it in his hand. There would be no way he was going to allow Greed to escape his impending demise.

"Nigga, I'm sendin' you to your muthafuckin' Maker!" he gritted.

He was sure this would end in a total victory. Not once did he consider that he might fail and Greed would escape his wrath. But even the best laid plans don't always bear ripened fruit.

King curled his lip and proceeded with his mission, only to encounter the totally unexpected.

Stay Connected with Us!

Text **LOCKDOWN** to 22828 to stay up-to-date with new releases, sneak peaks, contests and more...

Thank you!

Coming Soon from Lock Down Publications/Ca$h Presents

BOW DOWN TO MY GANGSTA

By **Ca$h & Jamaica**

TORN BETWEEN TWO

By **Coffee**

BLOOD OF A BOSS **IV**

By **Askari**

BRIDE OF A HUSTLA **III**

By **Destiny Skai**

WHEN A GOOD GIRL GOES BAD **II**

By **Adrienne**

LOVE & CHASIN' PAPER **II**

By **Qay Crockett**

THE HEART OF A GANGSTA **II**

By **Jerry Jackson**

LOYAL TO THE GAME **IV**

By **T.J. & Jelissa**

A DOPEBOY'S PRAYER **II**

By **Eddie "Wolf" Lee**

TRUE SAVAGE **III**

By **Chris Green**

IF LOVING YOU IS WRONG… **II**

By **Jelissa**

BLOODY COMMAS **III**

By **T.J. Edwards**

A DISTINGUISHED THUG STOLE MY HEART **II**

By **Meesha**

ADDICTIED TO THE DRAMA **II**

By **Jamila Mathis**

<u>Available Now</u>

<u>RESTRAINING ORDER</u> **I & II**

By **CA$H & Coffee**

<u>LOVE KNOWS NO BOUNDARIES</u> **I II & III**

By **Coffee**

<u>RAISED AS A GOON I, II & III</u>

By **Ghost**

<u>LAY IT DOWN</u> **I & II**

<u>LAST OF A DYING BREED</u>

By **Jamaica**

<u>LOYAL TO THE GAME</u>

<u>LOYAL TO THE GAME II</u>

LOYAL TO THE GAME III

By **TJ & Jelissa**

BLOODY COMMAS

By **T.J. Edwards**

IF LOVING HIM IS WRONG...

By **Jelissa**

A DISTINGUISHED THUG STOLE MY HEART

By **Meesha**

PUSH IT TO THE LIMIT

By **Bre' Hayes**

BLOOD OF A BOSS **I II & III**

By **Askari**

THE STREETS BLEED MURDER **I, II & III**

THE HEART OF A GANGSTA

By **Jerry Jackson**

CUM FOR ME

CUM FOR ME 2

CUM FOR ME 3

An **LDP Erotica Collaboration**

BRIDE OF A HUSTLA **I & II**

THE FETTI GIRLS **I, II& II**

By **Destiny Skai**

T.J. Edwards

WHEN A GOOD GIRL GOES BAD

By **Adrienne**

A GANGSTER'S REVENGE **I II III & IV**

THE BOSS MAN'S DAUGHTERS

THE BOSS MAN'S DAUGHTERS II

A SAVAGE LOVE **I & II**

BAE BELONGS TO ME

A HUSTLER'S DECEIT I, II

By **Aryanna**

A KINGPIN'S AMBITON

A KINGPIN'S AMBITION **II**

I MURDER FOR THE DOUGH

By **Ambitious**

TRUE SAVAGE

TRUE SAVAGE II

By **Chris Green**

A DOPEBOY'S PRAYER

By **Eddie "Wolf" Lee**

WHAT ABOUT US **I & II**

NEVER LOVE AGAIN

THUG ADDICTION

By **Kim Kaye**

THE KING CARTEL **I, II & III**

By **Frank Gresham**

THESE NIGGAS AIN'T LOYAL **I, II & III**

By **Nikki Tee**

GANGSTA SHYT **I II &III**

By **CATO**

THE ULTIMATE BETRAYAL

By **Phoenix**

BOSS'N UP **I & II**

By **Royal Nicole**

I LOVE YOU TO DEATH

By Destiny J

I RIDE FOR MY HITTA

I STILL RIDE FOR MY HITTA

By **Misty Holt**

LOVE & CHASIN' PAPER

By **Qay Crockett**

TO DIE IN VAIN

By **ASAD**

BOOKS BY LDP'S CEO, CA$H

TRUST IN NO MAN

TRUST IN NO MAN 2

TRUST IN NO MAN 3

BONDED BY BLOOD

SHORTY GOT A THUG

THUGS CRY

THUGS CRY 2

THUGS CRY 3

TRUST NO BITCH

TRUST NO BITCH 2

TRUST NO BITCH 3

TIL MY CASKET DROPS

RESTRAINING ORDER

RESTRAINING ORDER 2

IN LOVE WITH A CONVICT

Coming Soon

BONDED BY BLOOD 2

BOW DOWN TO MY GANGSTA